A Brain
in Third Person II

The Return of The Bad Penny

ISBN-13: 978-0-9994538-3-4
ISBN-10: 0-9994538-3-1

First printing: August 2018

Cover design by ThomasMax
Photo of Mr. Etter with B.J. by Lee Clevenger

Front-cover "bad penny" illustration (also shown on second title page) furnished by Shaun Hughes Hand Engraving UK. Used with permission. See his process on YouTube at:
https://www.youtube.com/channel/UCE2rGFm1-xs-WIEHfY1enjA

Published by:

tm

ThomasMax Publishing
P.O. Box 250054
Atlanta, GA 30325
www.thomasmax.com

A Brain in Third Person II

The Return of The Bad Penny

A. Shane Etter

ThomasMax

Your Publisher
For The 21st Century

ACKNOWLEDGMENTS

I'd like to thank my mentor, two-time Pulitzer nominee, Jedwin Smith. This is number five with your help and they wouldn't happen without you. Thank you.

Jedwin introduced me to Chuck Clark, a great editor. Thank you for your magic, Chuck. Thank you to the members of our ongoing Writer's Workshop. You're tough on me, challenge me and make me better. I know I don't always show it, but I appreciate it.

Thank you, Charles Clifford Brooks, III, founder of The Southern Collective Experience, my brother from another mother. Thank you for your friendship, your inspiration, for believing in me and everything you do.

To my sister, Amy Mills and my brother, CW5 U.S. Army, (Ret), Kevin A. Etter, thank you for a lifetime of love and support. I hit the jackpot with both of you.

Thanks to all my friends, old and new, writers and non-writers who have supported me in both words and actions. I will always be grateful.

Thank you to all the great writers I read for making me better, even though you don't know you're doing it.

Thank you again, Lee Clevenger of Thomas Max Publishing, for believing in "Return."

For Bonni Newberry
for all you give

OTHER BOOKS
BY A. SHANE ETTER

Bottom Dwellers

Mind Dwellers

Trail Dwellers

A Brain in Third Person

A War in The Bronx

*A Brain in Third Person II
– The Return of The Bad Penny*

Chapter One
Forgiven

Having realized less than an hour before that Bad Penny, his murderous alter ego, had departed from him, Pennington Wentworth II became suddenly aware that for the better part of a year he had been a different person, one who'd killed twelve people. He asked the super-sized prison guard he'd come to know over the past few weeks if he could use the payphone. It was after 5 p.m., but he hoped Ben Wasserman would answer at the cottage where he was staying on the prison grounds, for attorneys, spiritual advisors and family members of those whose execution was eminent. Since he was only about twelve hours away from being killed legally by the great state of Georgia it was an important call that could have life-saving consequences.

The Georgia Diagnostic and Classification Center was Georgia's most important prison, and where all new prisoners were sent for medical, psychological and mental testing. It housed a general population for those who would stay for the long term and a death row unit for those who had a short term wait before execution, where Bad Penny had been for the last month.

He pulled out his last quarter, examined it fearfully and angrily and hoped it would be the last quarter he'd ever have to use to make a phone call. He'd be on the outside soon using the latest and greatest cell phone again.

Someone answered, and seeing on the switchboard that the call was coming from within the prison grounds, said not impolitely, "How can I help you?"

"Hello. This is Pennington Wentworth the II. Is Mr. Wasserman available by any chance?"

"I think he's in his room, Mr. Wentworth. Can I give him a message?"

"Thank you, my dear. Yes, you may. Could you please tell him I'm back?"

"You're back?"

"Forgive me. What I mean is tell him that Bad Penny's gone. I'm back." Then, trying to keep it lighthearted, "I'm sorry. I know you don't understand. There's no way you could. Nothing urgent—I just need to see if there's anything he can do to stop my execution in the morning."

"Oh dear. I suppose I should give you his cell number."

"Could you possibly forward my call, dear lady? I'm on a pay phone in the prison and just used my only quarter." *How embarrassing that was.*

"I can try, Mr. Wentworth. Please hold."

Transferring, the ring changed tones. A moment later, "Ben Wasserman."

"Mr. Wasserman, it's Pennington.'

"Pennington, what can I do for you?"

'Bad Penny, he's gone."

"What?"

"He's gone. I'm back. I can remember everything he did, but he is gone. I know it sounds crazy, but it's like he was someone else inhabiting my body, and now he's disappeared. A veil has been lifted from me. Is there anything you can do?"

Immediately convinced of Pennington's sincerity by the difference he heard in his tone, language and respectfulness, Wasserman said,"Well, it sounds like I need to call the Governor's office, get him to 'stay' the execution, an appeal hearing before a judge, and get your conviction vacated. Then maybe all those protestors outside the gate will go home. Night before an execution, there's at least a couple of hundred of them, maybe more, out there, chanting and singing. It seems like you've created quite a stir."

"Oh, dear me. That's the last thing I want to do. I don't want to make trouble for anyone. Thank you, Counselor. I'd be grateful if you could." Pennington had changed his refrain as the hours counted down. He now hoped that he could live.

***

Ben clicked off and Googled the telephone number for the governor's office on the iPad Pro he kept in a side pocket of his briefcase. For situations like this he wished he'd programmed the number into his phone, but he could recall only one other time he'd called the powerful man's office. Fortunately, the state, in its infinite wisdom, had provided effective Wi-Fi on the prison grounds. Finding the number, he placed the call and told the after-hours staff it was a life saving emergency. They agreed to call the governor and the most important man in the Great State of Georgia put the wheels in motion.

Delaying the execution was relatively easy. The current governor, although a Republican, was left of center on social issues and this was one that fell under that heading. Then the heavy lifting began. To convince himself that his client was ingenuous Ben had to understand what Pennington was experiencing, so that he could convince a judge that an entirely different entity had committed the murders, an entity that no longer existed…or at least didn't inhabit Ben's client.

Ben and Pennington reached the conference room at the same time. Pennington was escorted by another giant of an armed guard. And because Bad Penny's attitude—his swagger—was gone, Ben thought he looked smaller.

"How're you holding up, Pennington?" Ben asked as he retrieved a yellow legal pad from his briefcase and a platinum Mont Blanc rollerball pen from his suit jacket's inside chest pocket. He added, "You know, I hate wearing this damn thing. Monkey suits have just about gone the way of the dodo bird. Like station wagons. It seems only attorneys and bankers wear them—and the President, but he doesn't wear a tie with his. Sorry; I got off track there for a second."

"I'm scared to death, Mr. Wasserman. I won't survive in this place. Please. You've got to do something."

"Believe me, Pennington. I'm already on it. But in the meantime, I need you to tell me everything that happened. Don't omit a single detail."

"Well, I went to dinner last night. Although, I really shouldn't call it dinner. It's not like I had wine or multiple courses. Alas, I digress. I went for supper and the server, God bless him, as usual, put my three hamburgers on the tray and I looked at them and just felt sick, even though I've been eating beef for months. And I just knew he was gone."

"Bad Penny, you mean? Bad Penny was gone?" Ben took notes as he questioned him. Sometimes he used his iPad. Now, he chose to handwrite his notes. He felt like he could better connect with them mentally and God knew he needed to connect with them as well as possible.

"Yes, Bad Penny."

"Anything else Pennington?"

"As I mentioned, I'm scared to death in this place. And I'd like some better clothes. This prison uniform—it doesn't do a thing for me. Stripes make me look fat, and I'd like a private bathroom. I mean, I was too scared to even take a shower this morning. Of course if it were possible I'd love to have a tub for a bath. I won't survive in here. I'm not like these men. They're animals, heathens, thugs." He was on the verge of tears and wringing his hands.

There was a pronounced change in Pennington that would be obvious to anyone with half a brain and knew Bad Penny. He'd returned to his passive, weak, effeminate, and meek-as-a-lamb true persona.

And then, tears erupted. "Can't you do something, Mr. Wasserman?"

Ben patted him on the shoulder. "Now, now, Pennington, calm yourself. At the very least I'm hoping I can get you moved out of death row. I'll make a call as soon as I leave." After his client gave him all the other information he could think of, Ben began to repack his briefcase. "Try to keep your head down until I can do something."

"Thank you, Mr. Wasserman. I'll do my best," he said, wiping his runny nose and teary eyes on the prison uniform sleeve, then looked at it, trying to remember how old he was the last time he'd done that.

Pennington's politeness, without smartassery or even a hint of attitude or arrogance, surprised Ben. In their previous dealings, Ben could clearly see the cocky bravado on Pennington's face, mixed with attitude, and hear it in every syllable he uttered.

Back in his room, Ben placed a call to the prison switchboard and asked for the warden, Mr. Oliver Henry.

"Mr. Henry, Ben Wasserman, attorney for Pennington Wentworth the second, here. As I know you're aware, I got his execution delayed."

"Yeah, I know who you are." The attorney could tell from the man's tone that the warden felt he was interfering. Not a surprise coming from the CEO of a prison. He'd encountered it before.

"Well, anyway, I believe he's a different person. The man who committed the murders doesn't exist any longer."

"What do you mean, doesn't exist? You mean like a multiple personality?" Ben could hear the skepticism.

"Something like that. Anyway I believe I can get his conviction overturned. And until then I need to get him out of the execution wing."

"Tell it to the judge, Ben. That can only be done with a court order."

"Okay then. You'll hear from me. Or the judge."

"All right, then. You take care now."

Ben disconnected the call and with Judge William Stephens' office number programmed into his phone he touched his name on the screen and heard the call connect.

"Judge Stephens' office, this is Suzanne. How can I help you?"

Ben had been in the judge's office often enough to remember his cute, blond secretary and her great legs and short skirts. He would've been interested if all his visits hadn't been for business. "Hi, Suzanne. This is Ben Wasserman. Wondering when's the soonest I could see the Judge in his chambers."

"What's this regarding Mr. Wasserman?"

"Getting Pennington Wentworth, II moved off death row."

"Hmmm, I see. Judge Stephens has an hour open tomorrow afternoon at 2:00. Will that do?"

"Sure will. Thank you, Suzanne. I'll be there at two tomorrow."

"I'll write you in, then."

"Thank you. Bye now."

"Good-bye, Mr. Wasserman."

***

"Good afternoon, Mr. Wasserman."

"Good afternoon."

The judge is expecting you. I'll let him know you're here."

"Thank you, Suzanne."

Picking up the phone. "Mr. Wasserman is here. Yes, Judge."

To Ben, "You may enter."

The judge's dark wood paneled office, was in stark contrast to the rest of the unattractive, postmodern, yellow brick government building.

"Ben, come in, come in." The judge rose, shook Ben's hand and gestured for him to sit in one of the two leather armchairs fronting his oversize desk. Exactly like you'd expect in a high-profile judge's office: Dark brown leather that smelled expensive and of leather conditioner, with brass nail heads on the seams. The judge wore the bow tie that was the defining icon of his carefully cultivated image. This one was Navy blue with white pin dots.

"Thank you, Judge."

"So, how can I be of help?"

"You remember my client, Pennington Wentworth, the second."

"Of course. My memory isn't what it used to be but it's not that far gone yet, knock on wood." He rapped his knuckles against the side of his head as he tilted it.

"Judge, I don't know if you're aware of it, but the governor stayed his execution. I need to get him removed from the execution wing."

"Well, Ben, I need more information."

The attorney withdrew a manila folder from his briefcase and pushed it across the polished surface of the judge's fanatically neat worktop. Everyone who knew him knew that he was obsessive about keeping his desk free from clutter. "Here's my request to the court in hard copy. It has all the details, so I won't bore you with them now. But just so you're aware, I'll be filing paperwork for an appeal. Got to get that conviction overturned."

Judge Stephens cleared his throat unceremoniously . It was a non-verbal reply his faculty advisor had taught him to do when he didn't want to give an answer that might come back to haunt him.

Ben stood and the judge raised half-way from his chair and offered his hand.

"Thank you, Judge. I don't want to take anymore of your time."

"You're very welcome, Ben. You can call for my decision anytime tomorrow afternoon."

"Thank you, again, your Honor."

***

Not wasting any more time than necessary, but still giving him time to return from lunch, Ben called Judge Stephens' office at 1:15. Suzanne answered, "Judge Henry is expecting your call. Hold please."

Barry Manilow's "Mandy" playing through to the end while he was on hold told him how long he waited. *This can't be good. He probably feels like he should tell me himself because he's denying the request. Or maybe he wants to give me good news. Who the hell knows?*

"Ben, how are you?"

"You tell me, Judge. How am I? More importantly, how's my

client?"

"You get right to the point, don't you, Ben? I like that about you. But, I'm sorry. I have to deny your request to remove Mr. Wentworth from the execution wing." It was grimly humorous that they both referred to it by its most formal name. Usually, everyone called it "death row."

"I'm sorry too, Judge. And with all due respect, I must say I respectfully disagree with your decision."

"You're allowed to disagree with me, Ben, as long as it's respectfully." The judge was trying to be amusing and he chuckled as soon as he'd said it. "But, if you're successful in getting a conviction appeal scheduled, I'll reconsider at that time."

"Well, thank you for that, your Honor. I'll be in touch."

"I'll look forward to it."

Chapter Two
Decontructing Pennington

Trying not to be too obvious about it, Pennington made inquiries into who could help him survive. More to the point: who was the Georgia Diagnostic and Classification Prison's oldest, longest surviving inmate?

It wasn't hard to figure out. The prison was a small community. He was led to Jon Schmidt, known to his minions, the ones who did his bidding, by the name that he ordered them to use, that he'd given himself—Orpheus. Most inmates didn't know his given name.

Wanting to be respectful and because his own shadow nearly frightened him to death, Pennington requested a meeting with Orpheus using the proper inmate channels. His followers and sycophants were known by the small braided brown leather bracelets worn on their right wrists. That and their physical stature. They were the biggest, baddest motherfuckers in the prison. They would only shake hands with their lefts because their right hands, the ones with which they would inflict the most damage, if need be, belonged to Orpheus.

Orpheus accepted his request for an audience three days hence, only because he'd heard of and been intrigued by the man known as The Bad Penny. "The" having been added to Pennington's sobriquet, as homage by other inmates, as his reputation grew.

Making his way to the door of Orpheus' "office," the soft strains of a sad melody from a stringed instrument floated on the air. Orpheus had fashioned the lyre himself from scrap wood obtained on his behalf in the prison workshop as an outlet for his woodworking creativity. He chose the lyre because it was the instrument his namesake used to charm animals and people. He played it now as a channel for his lyrical, musical passion. To earn his good graces inmates would take almost any risk to get him anything he required and if they were unable to, guards eager to curry his favor, would get what he wanted because all knew he was the de facto head of the institution.

"Sir, thank you sir, for seeing me." Pennington bowed as he approached Orpheus' throne, a handmade highbacked wooden chair in a broom closet. No longer The Bad Penny, he was scared shitless.

"Nonsense. How may I help you?" Though not as kind as the great wizard himself, Orpheus' proper speech and practiced good manners reminded one of The Lord Of The Ring's Gandalf.

Orpheus had to admit to himself that The Bad Penny was not what he'd expected. His reputation had preceded him and in no way did the young fellow seem like the type that could murder twelve people on the outside and two more—one of them a huge, badass latino—here on the inside.

"I'm not what I was. Or I guess I should say I'm back to what I was."

Orpheus tilted his head in honest confusion. "Please explain if you will, and take your time."

Pennington told him all he could, all he remembered about his previous life—the automobile accident, becoming The Bad Penny and all it involved. He ended his tale by relating to Orpheus that he had money—millions—and could take care of Orpheus' family, his wife and, children and grandchildren if the man would but help him survive his prison stay until he was released and able to get to the fortune.

"How about one million dollars, and as a show of good faith," Pennington said, "I can have $100,000 wired to your wife immediately. My attorney can take care of it for me." Pennington figured a million dollars—not three per cent of his nest egg—for his life, was a good investment.

Unable as he was to take care of his family, Orpheus quickly paid attention.

"That's quite a story, Penny. So, again, how can I help you?

"I'm asking you—no—pleading with you, sir, to help me survive. I mean, I'm not 'The Bad Penny' any longer, and without your help I won't make it in here."

Pennington was begging now. "Please, can you help me?"

"I'm sure I can, but it won't be easy. We will have to deconstruct Pennington and reconstruct The Bad Penny."

"What will we do? Lift weights, karate, judo, boxing?"

"By all means, all of those, but first, philosophy, aesthetics, history, science."

"But, how will those things help me survive?"

"The great Greek philosophers, Socrates, who in succession taught Plato, who in turn taught Aristotle, not only believed in a strong body, but a strong mind as well. So, we will start with their principles, build the mind, the spirit and the body, and you will become a formidable man, a formidable opponent, if need be, in all areas and in every arena."

"Then I shall trust you, Orpheus. But I just need this to happen quickly before someone kills me."

"That has already been taken care of." Orpheus smiled, nodding to the two large, well-muscled henchmen lurking and listening nearby. We will begin your studies tomorrow."

"I'm ready if you are."

"Fine. Fine. And in the meantime rest easy because my men will be shadowing you, watching over you, to keep you alive until you can take care of yourself once again.

Next day after lunch, Pennington would return to the closet to meet with his new mentor.

***

After first knocking, then being allowed into Orpheus' receiving room, Pennington bowed as he slinked meekly into the important man's personal space.

Orpheus spoke. "Welcome."

"Yes sir, thank you, sir." Pennington said, bowing again.

"Sit," Orpheus gently commanded.

On a three-foot by three-foot square of hand-cut, hand-trimmed carpet Pennington did as he was told, crossing his legs and straightening his spine to sit Indian-style.

"And, sir, I have a call into Mr. Wasserman—that's my attorney— to send your wife a check for that initial payment of one-hundred thousand dollars."

"Thank you, young man. Then let's proceed with your study."

Without further prelude, Orpheus began, "Socrates was a brilliant man who lived from 470 or 469 to 399 B.C; and although historians know the year of his demise—after he was sentenced to death for failing to acknowledge the Gods of Greece and corrupting the youth of Athens—by drinking hemlock, they are unsure of the year of his birth. We start with the first, although he was succeeded by his student, Plato, and he in turn by his, Aristotle, who history generally regards as the greatest philosopher ever.

For Socrates, philosophy was a lifelong quest, a path to be followed above all others, nay, the only path. He felt no other path was necessary. He wed but tended to fall in love with handsome young men, which means he would have loved it in here." Orpheus smiled bemusedly as he pondered that thought.

Continuing, "Socrates was short, thickly built and an unclean man. He liked wine and intelligent conversation and the latter is why he enjoyed teaching the wealthy young men of Athens—that and the previously mentioned penchant for handsome young men."

"But Orpheus, sir," Pennington interrupted, "excuse me, sir, but how is this going to keep me alive, help me survive with all the bad asses in this place?" And he cast his gaze around the room as if he could see through the walls.

"Dear Bad Penny, have patience. Socrates thought wisdom and intelligence were the greatest of virtues, above even the law, worthy of their own rewards. But he also served in the Athenian army and was, by all accounts, a strong man and was himself, quite formidable. So if we take his teachings not as a monolith, but as discrete and separate tenets, we can tie them to the physical, the strengths of man and make you in turn, stronger and formidable."

"Well, that certainly sounds compelling. I'll have to have faith in you."

"Thank you, young man, and you shall be rewarded for it. But, let us continue."

Orpheus regaled Pennington with the fiction-like tales of Socrates, as recorded by Plato and Aristotle, since as far as history can discern, Socrates never put on paper his thoughts and teachings, preferring to present his ideas in the form of debates and conversations.

At the conclusion, Orpheus queried: "So, I shall see you tomorrow, same time?"

"I have nowhere else to be, so, unless I'm dead, I'll be here."

"Well, unless my men aren't as good as I think they are—and they are—that won't be the case. Thank the Good Lord." And Orpheus made the sign of the cross, and in the way of latinos, kissed his thumbnail as the last part of the holy movement. Pennington, now the faithful student, crossed himself as well.

"Amen."

Chapter Three
Reconstruction

As Pennington opened the door to exit, Orpheus said, "Feel free to work out on your own. The mind-body-spirit connection cannot be denied, and after our studies I'm confident that your physical body will be stronger and your workout will be of even greater benefit to you, building more muscle and to make you robust and intrepid."

Pennington, in the way of martial artists, dipped from the shoulders only and bowed tersely then strode toward his cell to work out.

Once in his small living space, from a standing position, Pennington dropped to the concrete floor, stopping his fall by landing on the palms of his hands and was able to knock out thirty push-ups in one set. The most he'd done in a single set since the hundreds he'd do before The Bad Penny left him. Indeed, he thought, Orpheus certainly knew what he was doing with the whole mind, body, spirit connection thing.

It seemed, while he worked out in his cell, as if his swagger were returning after his studies. Of course, increasing the number of push-ups he did didn't hurt with that, either. He felt like he wouldn't even have to rehearse the swagger; it would just happen.

He got to test his theory when he went to supper. He walked to the food line and, without conscious effort, he felt a bit of the cockiness return. He didn't know if it would last or if it only worked for a few hours after his sessions with Orpheus, while his brain was open to it, but he was pleased with even small steps. The muscle he built with each push-up, he knew would endure. He only wished he still had the taste for beef that The Bad Penny enjoyed, to aide in the muscle-building.

He picked up his tray from the silver rails and walked with a purpose to his usual table. Even the innocent and naïve Pennington Wentworth II could figure out that there was strength in numbers and he'd probably be safer at the table with his Caucasian "friends." And thus far, they hadn't appeared to notice his change, or they were at least kind enough to not mention it, although "kind" wasn't a word he would ascribe to any of the convicted criminals. And besides, there was no escaping The Bad Penny's murderous reputation. So, he figured they probably thought it best not to take a chance with him, even if he didn't appear as aggressive as before.

The inmate entrusted with book distribution rolled by the cell doors pushing a library cart. Bad Penny usually waved him off, but this time Pennington asked if he had any books on philosophy. The guard told him he did and passed him a thin book, less than two hundred pages, titled *Aristotle For Everyone, Difficult Thought Made Easy* by Mortimer J. Adler. It was the perfect read because, as Orpheus said, Socrates taught Plato, who taught Aristotle and he could receive the teachings handed down from the first two by studying the third alone.

Pennington figured something simple would be a good place to start, even though when he was in college he'd felt like philosophy courses were too elementary and only those with little ambition would dare pursue it as a major. But now he was grateful someone had thought to donate the book to the prison.

He and Orpheus met again the next day. Pennington still showed deference and respect to his teacher, even though Orpheus showed him equal respect.

"So how's it going, Pennington?"

"Pretty well, but I haven't seen your men shadowing me."

"And you never will. But don't torment yourself. I give you my word—they're there".

Orpheus paused, then said, "You know, Penny, we have started with the Greek philosophers, but that's only the beginning. Once we've finished with them we'll move on to the Eastern philosophers and last, but certainly not least, the Romans."

"Whatever you say, sir. I'm with you."

"Fine, then let's get to it. The Greeks were warriors and that warrior-attitude permeated their society, their lives, their very existence. Without the warrior spirit they weren't Greeks. So, that's where we will take your education, although, an abbreviated course of study to imbue you with that warrior spirit as quickly as possible."

The warrior spirit…Pennington mulled that concept.

It would have been terrible if The Bad Penny had had that warrior spirit when he was on his rampage. It was bad enough as it was. Now that his meek self had returned and remembered what he'd done he could hardly live with himself.

***

For the next three months, or season, as the Greeks would have measured it, Pennington continued his study of philosophy and became quite adept at the teachings of the big three.

At the end of that season, Orpheus started him on the way-of-the-empty hand, or karate, as it is spoken in Japanese. As Orpheus continued to tear down Pennington, creating in turn a space for The Bad Penny to be recreated, Pennington grew, opening his mind for karate, kung-fu, escrima. and other martial arts of the east. That was also a good time to start the study of Eastern philosophers.

With practically an entire adult life spent incarcerated, Orpheus had had plenty of time to read, study, and acquire a complete knowledge on subjects he had only touched on with his somewhat limited formal education. It had been said that if one reads only five books on a given subject that that person would be more knowledgable than ninety-nine percent of the people on the planet on that subject. Orpheus had read thousands of books on dozens of subjects, making him a veritable expert of experts on martial arts, philosophy, math, medicine, psychology, history and the human brain. And he even harbored a dream of writing a novel, drawing on all his areas of knowledge that would be his legacy to the world before his demise in this hellhole, that he knew would be his ignominious ending.

In training Pennington in karate, Orpheus started with its beginnings on Okinawa, the sixty-two-mile-long island where karate was conceived, practiced and honed until it was sent out as a gift to the rest of the world, by way of the US military men who had been stationed on that island.

Orpheus showed Pennington how to show proper respect, teaching him to bow, to remove his shoes before entering the place of practice, and the proper use of the title, *sensei*, which even though it's what one calls their teacher, actually translates in Japanese to "one who came before."

"So, Sensei, when will I learn how to punch?"

"In due time, dear boy, in due time. But first you must learn bushido—the code of conduct of the samurai, the warrior."

Orpheus continued, "Bushido is based on seven important principles: seigi-the right decision and rectitude; yuki-bravery and heroism; jin-compassion and benevolence; reigi-courtesy; makoto-truthfulness and sincerity; meiyo-honor and glory; chugi-devotion and loyalty. Once you have grasped these principles you will be ready to learn combat." Pennington took note of the code of bushido in a composition book Orpheus provided him since neither pen nor proper paper were allowed inmates through the usual channels. And even though Orpheus wasn't bound by such mundane rules, and in fact as the de-facto head of the prison made his own rules and the ones that everyone else—both inmates and prison officials, followed.

"Thank you, Sensei." Pennington bowed, his forehead touching the floor from where he sat on his knees on a small mat in front of Orpheus' chair.

"Very good," said Orpheus. "I encourage you to study these on your own until you're able to recite them to me without referring to your notes. Etch each of them into the granite of your gray matter." Orpheus had decided he would have liked Pennington even if he didn't have an affinity for handsome young men. He felt like there was a lot to like about the person inside the attractive body.

The next day Pennington bowed upon entering Orpheus' sanctuary. His mentor said, "Recite for me your code. You may read from your notes, if you like."

However, to Orpheus' surprise, Pennington was able to recite them by rote with only minor hesitation.

Orpheus applauded, "Outstanding, young fellow. These words must be your creed. Words you must live by; both on the inside and later on the outside. They will serve you well, Nay, very well, indeed."

"Thank you, Sensei. And an interrogatory, if I may: What does bushido mean to you?"

"I have a better idea. Why don't you tell me what it means to you?"

Pennington looked thoughtful. "I need to improve my decision-making process. I should be courteous to everyone in all dealings with them. Heroism means I should be heroic and honorable in my actions, even when no one is watching. And I'm still considering the other concepts."

"Outstanding, dear boy. I think you're on to something."

"Well, I'm not yet sure I will be able to defend myself but I certainly am getting an education."

"Don't fret, dear boy. As I said, my men will watch over you, take care of you, until you can defend yourself. You have to remember—if The Bad Penny still existed in you, you could just go along as before, but you're not him any longer; he's not you; so we have to teach you the skills that were innately his. Besides we don't want you to be him any longer so you can get out of this God forsaken place."

Knowing the nature of Orpheus' crimes—molesting and ultimately killing a young boy, and seeing how much Orpheus seemed to enjoy the company of and education of Pennington— he felt like the man had more in common with Socrates than he was willing to admit. The other cons had noticed, and now Orpheus seemed fixated on Pennington's good looks, much like Socrates had noticed the handsome young Athenians. Only The Bad Penny's lethal reputation had ensured his survival, this despite his pretty-boy features.

Starting the lesson, Orpheus said, "All study of Eastern philosophy starts with Confucius, and ends...with Confucius. He believed that government could be based on the family, structured like the family."

"Another way to state it would be that he felt a government should govern using the natural morality of the people. He believed that most people were inherently good and therefore wanted to do what was right. He also had his own version of the Golden Rule we all know, which he stated as such. 'What one does not wish for oneself, one ought not to do to anyone else.' Notice how he emphasized, what one shouldn't do instead of what one should do. All this 500 years before Jesus of Nazareth, he said this before The Christ walked the earth."

"But with all due respect, Sensei, I don't see how the Golden Rule will keep me alive in here.

"Remember my young friend, it is my job to keep you alive until you can channel The Bad Penny again and take care of yourself." Orpheus stood. "And that's what we're going to do. I know it's easier said than done, but don't worry your head about it. And also, we're doing this to provide you a guidepost for the rest of your life. Oh, and by-the-by, I'm still pretty highly regarded in this disreputable pigsty. As long as I am and others know you're under my watch, most likely no one is going to accost you."

"I sure hope you're right, Sensei."

"I think you can count on it. Now, go get your workout and then eat big."

During the four hours before Pennington went to supper, he did four sets of twenty-five push-ups. He added bodyweight squats to his routine and hit the same numbers."

Elated over his improving numbers, he went to dinner and in spite of doubting himself as he entered the dining hall, emulated the Bad Penny swagger. He only hoped none of the other cons would be able to detect the conflict between machismo and meekness.

Joining his usual table, to the normal quiet but enthusiastic greetings, he thought he noticed a particularly tough-looking man in the food line paying an inordinate amount of attention to him. Pennington immediately assumed—and hoped—it was one of Orpheus' disciples watching over him, keeping him safe, but in the end he decided the man was not giving him undue attention and therefore wasn't necessarily a protector or someone to be feared—no more than anyone else in this place, anyway.

Pennington returned to his cell and after the lights went down the sounds of the night started. The farting, the sobbing, the moaning— from inmates jerking off, and then the worst—the sound of silence. He could handle all the rest easier than the quiet. He would have literally killed for a TV—he'd killed for less—or a radio in his cell, just as white noise.

Pennington went to breakfast the next morning and had scrambled eggs—he figured they were poured from a carton, but the bacon and sausage weren't bad, and about a gallon of black coffee. The coffee was burnt and stale. He figured it had first been burnt and then after no one wanted it, sitting there, it got stale. Nothing but protein and fats— no carbs—to keep him lean and building muscle.

The caffeine would fuel his workout since he wasn't getting carbs for an energy source.

***

After being told to enter Orpheus' chamber, upon knocking, then bowing and kneeling, Pennington said, "Domo arrigato, sensei," which contrary to popular belief didn't mean, "thank you, teacher", but translated in Japanese to "thank you, one who came before me."

"To continue from where we left off yesterday," Orpheus said, "Confucius was so important his name was given to an entire school of philosophy, Confucianism—it has had many adherents and many versions: Korean, Japanese, neo- and new-. To this day, current Confucians continue to teach and study. Ivanhoe and Neville followed the philosophy, and Ivanhoe had been critical of neo-Confucians' criticism of Buddhism and said that they were more influenced by that philosophy than they thought. Robert Neville has proposed that Confucianism should be a world philosophy and as an author of several important books devoted to Confucianism, has even been given a Chinese name—Nan Lo Shana."

They discussed the various branches of Confucianism and their importance: Korean, Japanese, neo and new. The Orpheus explained, "Korean Confucianism focused on four emotions: commiseration, shame, modesty, and integrity; and seven feelings: pleasure, anger, sorrow, fear, love, hatred, and desire. Yi T'oegye, one of the most prominent Korean Confucian scholars, felt that people entered into relationships with others and themselves based on these eleven concepts.

"And even in this God-forsaken place I believe we experience those seven feelings. Japanese Confucianism, on the other hand, seemed to have a more Western approach and one sees the word Ju used over and over again, referring to the Chinese version. The word means weakling in Japanese and they indeed thought that the Chinese sect focused only on the mental and not enough on the physical—hence the karate we know today one might see as an outgrowth of the physical manifestation of the Japanese Confucianism."

Pennington liked the idea that karate could be seen as an important part of philosophy.

They continued like this for weeks, Pennington soaking up the information like a proverbial sponge, and using the mind, body, spirit connection to power his workouts. Gradually he was becoming a real man again, but without the aggression or anger of The Bad Penny. The only thing that worried Pennington was when the thought crept into his head that had he been knowledgeable of martial arts previously, The Bad Penny would have been even more deadly. The fact that he could even think that was particularly worrisome to him and would have been to his victims as well.

***

A guard came to Pennington's cell. The guards could have as much attitude as cons. There probably wasn't much difference in them. Without destiny, or karma, the guards could have just as easily been cons. "Your attorney's here."

Knowing he was about to have his session with Orpheus, and displaying a little of the bluster that was The Bad Penny, he said, "I'm busy."

A redneck from South Georgia, the large caucasian guard, cloaked in attitude said, "Fine, no skin off my back, asshole."

Then, because it had been almost a month since they'd talked, Pennington decided it might be important that he see him.

"Allright, okay. I'll come with you."

"Don't knock yourself out. Like I said, I don't give a shit." And he really didn't. It was not possible for him to care any less.

The guard had the door unlocked and accompanied Pennington to the small room where Ben Wasserman was waiting for him. Pennington entered the room and glad-handed him. "Mr. Wasserman, how are you?" The Bad Penny had tended to use the attorney's first name for quite a while, but Pennington wanted to ensure that Wasserman had no doubts about his sweetness, his veracity, his sincerity and to have absolute belief that The Bad Penny was gone.

"Fine, Pennington. How are you?"

"Just fine, counselor, just fine. Doesn't mean I want to stay here, but I'm okay."

"Good. I'm happy to hear it. You know it's still three months until your hearing, but even so, we can't start too soon. Have you noticed any more changes in your brain, your personality, anything I need to know?"

"Nothing…except as you know, I'm studying with a gentleman in here, Orpheus—he really runs the prison—he's been teaching me philosophy. We're getting ready to start world history soon and he's helping me tremendously. He's a great mentor."

"That sounds real fine, Pennington. You're smart and I knew you'd begin to find your way in here. And, I'm not your financial adviser, but what's this about sending his wife a hundred K with the promise of a lot more.

"Well, sir, that was what we agreed my life's worth."

"What's that?"

"Orpheus really runs the prison and he and his men are going to keep me alive until you get me out of here."

"Well, you're obviously healthy, staying alive."

"Yes, thanks to Orpheus, I am, sir. He has his men watching over me, making sure no harm comes to me until I can handle myself; although I'm not sure that I'll ever be able to do that again. But to that end, he has started teaching me karate and I'm doing quite well, at least in the mental part of it. I'm really getting into the philosophy of the art instead of only the aggression and violence." Pennington felt he either had to bullshit him, or hold some things back from his attorney, convince him that The Bad Penny was not lurking somewhere in the dark recesses of his soul.

Pennington continued, "And, sir, if you need to see me more often, just to make sure we're on top of things, I'm at your beck-and-call, completely at your service." He laid it on thick; He was still Pennington, after all.

"Well, thank you, Pennington. We'll have to meet again, but probably not too often. Even though there are things that make your case unique, it's not my first barbecue, or my first rodeo, so I have a feeling—just a feeling, mind you—that we'll be okay."

"Thank the good Lord in Heaven, Mr. Wasserman. I don't know what I'll do if I have to be in here forever. Or worse, be executed."

"And I as well, Pennington. Even though I don't want you as a client in the future, I don't want to lose you."

Their conference finished, Wasserman picked up an internal phone and after speaking briefly with someone, a different huge guard collected Pennington, and left. With a fleeting thought, Wasserman wondered again where they found these behemoths.

Back in his SUV, the attorney couldn't escape the feeling of, or at least the hope, that he wasn't being played. Pennington seemed sincere, but something about it just didn't feel quite right.

Meanwhile, Pennington was having his own doubts. With his brain change from The Bad Penny, feeling permanent, Pennington felt like he was back to himself, except for the occasional fleeting thought, that he was frightened by what The Bad Penny could do again, if given the chance, and it worried him that he could even imagine what the other him could do.

But he was able to reassure himself by thinking that what The Bad

Penny did sounded so horrific that he couldn't possibly become The Bad Penny again and repeat those horrible types of crimes.

The following day Orpheus said, "Penny, I think it's time we start the serious study of martial arts." A moment later, the timing of the entry obviously planned, the baddest of his sycophants joined them in the small room.

"This is my friend, Gage; he is going to introduce you to the wonders of escrima, Kung fu, and expand on my rudimentary introduction to you of karate. Gage spent extended periods of time in Okinawa and the Philippines studying, respectively, the treasures of both of those island paradises—karate and escrima, also known as Kali."

As humble and as meek as ever, Pennington said, "Only if you think I'm ready, Sensei."

"No one is ever ready to begin the study of the martial arts. One must simply dive in and as one studies, one grows, and one's growth and learning become a monolith, gaining momentum, to eventually become an unstoppable force." Orpheus' education may have been mostly self-taught, but his depth of understanding of many subjects was comparable to many Ph.D.s, He wore a quiet arrogance borne out of self assurance that was both off putting and attractive. It was how he led a group of men who served his every wish. One was drawn to him and sought his approval; not only sought it, but required it and would do anything to get it.

Gage stood nearby; forty, he had the look of a hard man, physically and mentally, who'd seen much, spit in danger's eye, told it to kiss his ass and, survived. Nothing rattled him. His lean, sinewy arms crossed over his chest; a self-assured smirk gave life to an emotionless face. He wore black gi pants and a gray tank top. A boxer's hightop white ring shoes with red stripes incongruous with the karate pants and wife beater shirt. He was Orpheus' most-trusted bodyguard and had successfully kept his mentor and confidant safe.

He had the look of an undisturbed storm. Taking in everything, missing nothing, waiting until forced into action, not necessarily desiring it, but not yielding to it; ready and able to perform when needed.

"You may trust that Gage can teach you what you require. He spent a number of years in Okinawa, the birth place of karate, an amazing place and culture, because it gave the most popular martial art as a gift to the rest of the world. Then, my friend studied the escrima stick-fighting in its motherland, the Philippines and would most likely still be there had he not developed a...let's call it an unusual...prediliction...for young Filipinas—or was it all Asian women, Gage—not just Filipinas?" Gage glanced away as if in deep thought, as if remembering a pleasant thought, unwanting to be disturbed. Orpheus continued. "And although they were all bad, it caused him to be incarcerated in one of that country's worst island prisons, In fact, Pennington, the Philippines and this country's government have had a mutual defense treaty since World War II and my friend here almost single-handedly caused that agreement to be revoked. A remarkable feat for a lone man not in the employ of the federal government. And he would definitely still be a guest of their prison system had he not escaped, made his way to gain employment on a—let's call it—an unregistered, cargo ship providing carriage of goods of questionable legality, and making his way back to our country where he ended up in Atlanta. One might even come to the conclusion that the Pinoy government looked the other way when our friend here, escaped, preferring that he not be in their country at all. As it turned out there were a large number of Asian women in the ATL and once again, his unusual taste getting the best of him, he ended up in this shithole as a guest of the great state of Georgia."

"Gage, you may start where you think best with our young friend."

Gage bowed to Pennington—the habit developed in Southeast Asia, where the show of proper respect between martial artists, and, in fact, all people, was required, especially in that part of the world where humility and respect was fundamental—then stepped into the corner of the room and retrieved what looked like pieces of scrap wood. The two pieces of wood were about the length and size of batons, the rubber tipped pieces of metal, majorettes would have twirled in high school marching bands, they would use for their practice of escrima or kali.

"I prefer the name escrima over kali, from the original Filipino language, Tagalog, but you may call it either. Or even arnis, by which it is also known because of the large number of dialects spoken in the Philippines."

"Well, sir," Pennington said meekly, "If escrima is good enough for you then it's good enough for me." Pennington thought it was probably best not to piss off a badass like Gage, who was going to instruct him in martial arts. And he had to admit he was curious about just what the unusual taste for young Asian women the man had acquired, was.

Gage bowed again then handed Pennington one of the escrima sticks. It felt alien in his hand. Truth be known, he would have been more comfortable twirling it like a baton instead of using it to maim, or kill, an enemy. Gage shrugged. "It's up to you what you call them. Escrima sticks—or batons, the proper name, are typically twenty-six to twenty-eight inches long, so their length gives one the ability to strike from farther away than with the arm and a punch, or even one's leg, in a kick, but with escrima you will find that the practice and actual fighting is done in close quarters, no more than an arm's length away, because although you'll be striking and blocking with the stick, you will also be striking, and parrying with your free, empty hand. It's constant movement at all times with both of your upper extremities. It takes a great deal of coordination, which only comes with practice, hours and hours of practice."

Well, that's one thing I have plenty of—time."

Appearing inattentive, but eavesdropping, nonetheless, and just barely glancing up from the tome he was perusing, Orpheus said, "I'm glad you still have your sense of humor, my young friend, but hopefully you'll get that appeal and be out of this godawful shithole before long."

"From your lips to God's ear," said Pennington.

Gage said, "We're going to start with a few of the basic moves—strikes, blocks and parries."

"Whatever you think best, Mr. Gage."

"Not Mr. Gage. Just Gage, plain old Gage.

"Yes sir, Mr….ah…er…just Gage.

So Gage proceeded to show Pennington how to use both hands in tandem, his left for open hand blocks against Gage's open hand and how to intercept his baton with his own and deflect it without absorbing the full force.

Pennington was so focused that the hour passed quickly and at the end of the time he was drained, physically and mentally. Every square inch of his clothing drenched in sweat, probably for the first time in his life. Pennington Wentworth II had never been one to workout, or even work for that matter, in a manner that would produce perspiration.

Still unable to consume meat, at lunch Pennington asked for larger than normal servings of vegetables and beans, to try and substitute for the aversion to meat that he still felt since his mental return from The Bad Penny.

Sitting with his so-called *friends,* Pennington felt safe in the large dining room with them, but he couldn't imagine a life where he would have accepted these hooligans into his circle. His friends on the outside had been among Atlanta's high society, the ones always invited to the next function, the latest fund raiser or the newest opening. He couldn't wait to return to his former life.

After lunch, exhausted from his escrima workout, he returned to his cell and napped. He dreamed of his previous life, and also of murders, but not of murders that he'd committed, but ones he saw with himself as the killer, yet to be committed. He awoke frightened to tears. He'd scared himself with his nightmares, much like a novelist who frightens himself with his own make-believe stories.

***

"Enter, enter, my dear boy," Orpheus said in answer to Pennington's knock. He knew it was his student. Orpheus didn't get that many visitors unless he summoned them and most of those he did receive didn't knock. And those that did, were usually more aggressive in their banging.

Gage arrived a moment after.

"Splendid," said Orpheus, "You may commence."

Gage said, "We'll continue with our practice of the basics, adding some new techniques as we proceed."

Pennington acknowledged him with a curt head bob.

Although not aggressive in any way, and not a tough guy by any stretch of the imagination, it seemed that Pennington was taking to the rapid hand movements required in the practice of escrima. He could only attribute it to the fact that when in middle school and high school, he'd been a student conductor of the school's choral groups and it had trained his hands in coordination, making him more dexterous, which he felt was beginning to serve him well in the Filipino fighting art.

What most people didn't know is that unlike boxing, which is natural and requires less thought because of it's normal repetitive movements, most martial arts are not natural at all and require quick thinking and the ability to analyze one's opponent's moves quickly, to choose the right defensive technique and counter-attack. And if there was one thing Pennington had in spades, it was intelligence and a quick thought process. And if he were faking—if it were an act, that Pennington was back—or if it weren't permanent, with the fighting skills he was cultivating, he would be even deadlier. The city of Atlanta would once again be paralyzed with fear.

"I wish I could take the baton to practice in my cell," Pennington said.

Gage gave him a look as if he agreed, but Orpheus said, "We mustn't push our luck. I can get away with a good deal in here, but that would probably be a wee bit much even for me. The ones in uniform are serious about this being a prison and, although I've been here longer than he—our friend, the warden, still likes to think he's in charge, so let's allow him his delusions."

His hour of training over, Pennington departed for the dining room and along with his veggies, since it was Friday and the prison cooks were honoring the Catholic tradition of fish on the holy day, he made the decision to attempt to partake in some protein since he'd lost the Bad Penny's taste for red meat or even chicken.

A nap followed but without the nightmares from the previous day.

Gage continued to school him in the art of escrima for the better part of a month, with Orpheus testing him from time-to-time on the Greek, Roman and Asian philosophers and asking him to repeat the seven principles of bushido. As Orpheus said, "You must never overlook the mind, body, spirit connection."

After his high-speed course in escrima, Gage switched gears and started Pennington's training in Okinawan karate.

"The strength of karate is in kata and the basics," he told him in their first class. "It may be that you can make use of the fancy techniques, but never forget your friends, the front kick, sidekick, and roundhouse kick. Those—and the reverse punch, back fist and ridge hand—must become your best friends. If you're awakened in the middle of the night, they must be the first thing you think of—your immediate and natural reaction to whatever confronts you. Karate—the empty hand—must be second—no, first—nature to you. It must become as natural as breathing. So, we have a lot of work to do. And always remember: stay relaxed until you're not. In other words, stay relaxed until it's time not to be."

They started off doing front punches from a kiba dachi stance, in English known as a horse stance. In other words, standing with your knees bent and legs bowed, far apart, as if one were astride a horse. From the beginning, Gage gave Pennington commands and counted the repetitions in Japanese, demonstrating the commands at first, until Pennington understood them as well as in English.

Front punches, backfists, reverse punches from a square stance. Front kicks, sidekicks, roundhouse kicks; all broken down into four counts, slowing them down, breaking them into separate discrete parts of each technique. Imprinting them into his brain, so he would never forget, no matter the pressure, no matter the situation. When Gage launched kicks at Pennington the main thing that worried Pennington was he wasn't wearing a protective cup and the prospect of a kick to the nuggets made him nervous. But Gage had perfect focus and control and Pennington didn't need to worry.

After a few weeks of intense training, when Gage arrived early one morning, Orpheus said to him, "I hope our young friend's demons are truly gone, because with the progress he's shown, if he again becomes a killer, the city of Atlanta would be crippled by fear."

Having picked up the Filipino habit of not speaking, if a gesture, a nod or a look would suffice, Gage was not a man to waste words. A man of few words anyway, he just shrugged unsympathetically, like he didn't care one way or the other. And he probably didn't. All he knew was it didn't affect him.

The next session, like all of them, started with basics. He and Gage bowed to one another, then ippon kumite, or one point or first point fighting, which is controlled movement fighting, then Gage started teaching Pennington kata, pre-determined sets of moves, choreographed almost like a dance, to practice fighting multiple opponents.

"Remember," Gage said, "Some katas have been around for centuries. They are the essence of karate. Without kata, you have no soul. Without kata, karate is no different than any other kind of fighting. We would be nothing but animals without it."

Knowing Gage's background Pennington thought that was an

interesting thing for the man to say.

***

Waiting in line for breakfast the next morning, an inmate got pissed at Pennington for as he said, standing too close to him. Not sure if his lessons would work, but he didn't take time to worry about that; his training kicked in and he reacted without thinking. When the guy put his hands on Pennington's chest to shove him, the former Bad Penny pinned the guy's right hand to his chest with his left, then reaching over both of them with his right, braced it into an armbar, forcing him to the floor. But instead of breaking the appendage or dislocating his shoulder, he merely waited seconds for two of Orpheus' men to break up the set-to. It hadn't taken them long, seemingly out of nowhere, to appear.

By the time Pennington arrived for his karate training, always in the know about anything occurring in the prison, Orpheus had already received word.

"I understand there was an incident." He said raising the inflection on the last word, as if asking a question, awaiting confirmation.

"I'm sorry, Sensei." bowing as he apologized. "It's just that it happened so fast; I couldn't help it. I had to defend myself."

"I understand, my dear boy. I'm not angry with you. I'm just thankful you came through it unscathed. Apparently it happened so quickly none of my men could react before you did."

Gage entered almost on cue. "Hello my friend," Orpheus said. "Our young student had reason to use your teachings. Fortunately he's been paying attention, and he was able to dispatch the aggressor with alacrity."

"Fuckin' A", Gage said, in contrast to Orpheus' proper English and perfect diction, and extended a dramatically slow fist bump in Pennington's direction.

"Tell me what happened," said Gage.

So Pennington, both ashamedly and proudly, explained how he subdued the aggressor.

"Show me," Gage said. "So he put his hands on you like this, and what'd you do?"

Pennington demonstrated to Gage and Orpheus how he pinned the man's hand, bent his wrist back, twisting it into an arm bar and drove him into the floor.

From the ground, grimacing, Gage said, "Excellent. Excellent."

Orpheus: "Bravo."

Pennington was embarrassed at the attention from his teachers, but at the same time, proud of himself at how well he'd performed.

Climbing to his feet, Gage said, "So, let's get started."

"No time like the present," said Pennington.

Orpheus said, "It's obvious from the magnanimous way you handled your assailant that you've taken the code of bushido to heart and are indeed beginning to live its creed, but before we start today's training, let's recite it anyway, just to reinforce it. You must make sure it has taken root and has become a part of your DNA."

Pennington recited the seven points in the code of bushido.

"Fine. Fine." Orpheus said, when he'd finished, "We mustn't overlook the fundamentals." Gage looked on disinterestedly because all that interested him was the punching and kicking, not the philosophy.

***

Pennington's abbreviated but extremely intense training schedule continued for the next six weeks until his scheduled hearing.

The week prior to the hearing before the Georgia Conviction Appeals commission, Pennington's attorney, Ben Wasserman, having resumed his normal schedule at his office, called on him at the State of Georgia Diagnostic and Classification Prison. In the same attorney conference room of institutional tile, plastic and pale green walls, where they met previously.

Wasserman rose to shake hands with Pennington after the two guards departed. "How're you holding up?"

"As well as can be expected, Counselor. And you?"

"Fine, just fine. There's not a lot we need to discuss. I just wanted to check to see if it's still status quo. Any changes?"

"No, sir, about the same."

"Good, good. And although you'll be there, you won't have to do anything. In the great State of Georgia, the way you get a murder conviction vacated is for me to go before a commission—a seven-member panel: two judges of courts of record, selected by the Supreme

Court; three attorneys who have practiced law in this state for at least ten years, elected by the Board of Governors of the State Bar; and two citizens who are not members of the state Bar, appointed by the governor.

I then, must present your case and you don't have to do anything but be there, looking calm, normal and inexpressive. Just be yourself and you'll be fine."

"Thank you, Mr. Wasserman. I have to admit as the day draws nearer I'm getting a wee bit nervous. I mean, I'm doing okay, but I'm so ready to get back to my normal life. This has been an experience I wouldn't wish on my worst enemy."

"I understand, Pennington, and with God's help, and assuming I'm on top of my game—and I usually am— you'll be back in that penthouse of yours in no time at all."

"I can only pray you're right, sir."

"But one thing we have to do, is have a psychiatrist examine you, tomorrow, to make sure he agrees with us.

"I must say I'm not excited about getting my head shrunk, but if we must—"

"Believe me, Pennington, we must. It's very necessary."

"Alright then."

"Splendid. I've already spoken with our expert and he'll be here at ten o'clock tomorrow morning."

***

After meeting with his attorney, Pennington met Orpheus for an abbreviated session.

"Greetings, young man. Since we haven't in a while, why don't we talk about the big three Greeks a moment. Tell me; what in your opinion, are their greatest individual contributions?"

"Well, Sensei, Socrates didn't write his teachings, preferring teaching by asking probing questions, which has influenced generations. Plato, which wasn't his real name, by the way; it was Aristocles—he was quite an athlete, a champion wrestler and Plato came from a word for his massive shoulders, like plates of iron; his biggest contribution would be his book *The Republic,* where he put forth the idea that a philosopher should be king. Self-serving, I think, by the way.

"Aristotle was Plato's best student, his two largest accomplishments were that he tutored Alexander the Great and after starting his own school of philosophy, he wrote and produced almost one thousand books and pamphlets."

"Very good, my dear boy. Debatable but inarguable, which Socrates would appreciate, by the way. And how would you describe their relationships?"

"I would say that Aristotle, last of the three, but considered the greatest by history, was the philosophical scion of the two who preceded him."

"Splendid, Pennington, splendid. I've never heard it put so succinctly, yet so accurately. I'd say you've established yourself as a great philosophical intellect, who would make those monumental men proud. But, another question—which one affects you most profoundly, and why?"

"Thank you, Sensei. I can only dream. But, like most people since then, I must admit to caring most about Aristotle, due not entirely to, but nonetheless impressed by his teaching of the great warrior and leader, Alexander the Great."

"You don't think he was too pedantic?"

"With all due respect, Sensei, I don't think him at all pedantic. I just think he was a self-aware man, believed his views were accurate, and had the courage of his convictions."

Orpheus smiled. "Well, you've convinced me."

'Thank you, sir, and if what you say is in any way true, the credit belongs to you."

"Nonsense, my young friend. You put in the effort, you deserve the credit."

Chapter Four
Truth or Consequences

Doctor Kaplan arrived at 9:55 and the officer at the door of the interrogation room sent for Pennington.

"It's nice to meet you, Pennington. Mr. Wasserman has explained your case to me, but why don't you tell me your story."

"It's lovely to meet you, Doctor, but it's extremely difficult not only telling you what happened, but even thinking about it," his voice cracked, "because that's not me anymore." His brow was furrowed and he wrung his hands just in anticipation of telling his story.

"I understand, but why don't you give it a try, anyway?"

Pennington took a deep breath, his hands trembling and due to nerves, he checked his watch even though it couldn't have been more than three minutes after ten o'clock sharp, when he walked in. "I'll do my best. But, keep in mind, I didn't remember most of this for the longest time. I'm relying on the testimony of people who were said to be my friends, even though during the trial I had no recollection of them whatsoever."

Dr. Kaplan, entering notes of the comments in his iPad, nodded his understanding.

"Please go on, Pennington."

"I'll do my best, doctor," then proceeded to describe the massive pile-up on the connector in Buckhead and how he was transported to the emergency room at Grady Memorial Hospital.

"Apparently I was unconscious for two weeks, until—actually, it was the fifteenth day when I woke up. And this is where my memory crystallizes, at least some of what happened. I remember feeling pissed off at the world. Please forgive my language."

"Think nothing of it. I'm sure I, too, would have been pissed off at the world, as you so colorfully put it."

"Thank you, but it was just so unlike me." And this is where Pennington, after another deep breath, told him of his life previously.

"I was a sensitive child, and I guess, the truth be told, a wee bit effeminate, although I knew I wasn't gay, not that there's anything wrong with that. Please forgive me. I always liked that Seinfeld episode—but, I knew I liked girls at an early age."

"Please continue."

"Well, Doctor, that's why the brain injury was so shocking. It changed me completely; in ways no one could possibly have predicted."

"As I've gathered from the courtroom testimonies. So, describe for me how the aggression started. And committing the crimes."

Obviously distressed, he leaned forward with his elbows on his knees and his head in his hands. "Well, doctor, it's like I said, almost from the moment I woke up in the hospital, I was angry. I remember the physician, Doctor Watters, I believe was his name, and through no fault of his own, he's a fine man, and a superb physician, just annoyed me to no end and I wanted to do bodily harm to another human being. I've never been that way in my life and even now, more than a year later, I'm ashamed of my behavior and wish there were some way I could make it up to the doctor for the way I acted toward him, and atone for my sins, the crimes I committed—without being executed, of course. And I'm skipping around, but, speaking of sins, I'm worried about my eternal soul, since I murdered a Monsignor."

"We don't have to go in order, or even discuss them all. But please tell me about that one."

"Well, if I remember correctly, and I'm not sure I do, from the testimony, I mean, I think the monsignor was the fourth, but I remember this now from what I thought at the time—I was worried, that, even though reconciliation is supposed to be protected by the sanctity of the confessional, I was worried that he might tell someone and I decided I couldn't take that chance, so I killed him."

"Quite extraordinary—your line of thinking, that is. Killing a monsignor."

"Yes, Doctor. And I know how it sounds. I'm as disgusted saying it as you appear to be hearing it."

"I'm not here to judge, Pennington, simply to evaluate."

"I'm happy you don't judge, Doctor, but at this moment I'm worried about God's judgment. Good Lord," and he made the sign of the cross. "I murdered a high priest. I caved in his skull with a jewel-encrusted solid-gold chalice I stole from the altar, for God's sake. I mean, how can I even ask a priest to shrive me for killing another priest?"

"Well, Pennington, for right now let's just worry about the great State of Georgia's judgement and save God's for a later date."

Pennington shuddered and brushed away his tears. "Yes, I'd prefer that, sir," he said.

Dr. Kaplan administered a small battery of psychological tests to Pennington and, after two additional hours, decided that he had more than enough to make the decision that The Bad Penny had disappeared, or been vanquished and the man before him now was not the one who'd committed the heinous crimes for which he'd been convicted.

***

"Dr. Kaplan says, that in his judgement, Bad Penny is gone and you, my friend, are not the person who committed those murders." Ben Wasserman had shown up the day after his session with the psychiatrist without letting Pennington know ahead of time, just to judge his client's reaction. Pennington did not disappoint. He was thoroughly pleased with the shrink's assessment, but he was privately miffed because it took him away from his studies with Orpheus.

"So, I believe we're ready for the hearing. I just need you to show up on time and come dressed to play."

"I'll do my best, Mr. Wasserman."

"I know you will, Pennington. And just so you know, I feel real good about this."

"Then I'm confident, if you're confident, Counselor."

***

The Conviction Appeals Commission met in one of the several courtrooms in the Georgia State Supreme Court building in downtown Atlanta. Unlike traditional courtrooms, it was set up to accommodate the seven members of the commission instead of a single judge, and space for law assistants, all attorneys licensed in the State of Georgia, who were there to do whatever the commission members might require of them. The defendant's table was typical, roomy enough for the attorney and the appellate and their needs.

Ben Wasserman arrived early and was placing his notes, notebooks and iPad at his fingertips on the table's top. Before he was done arranging his items, the door to the courtroom opened. Two burly officers entered, escorting Pennington.

"Good morning, Counselor," he said, sheepishly.

"Good morning, Pennington. Thank you, officers," he said.

"We'll be at the rear of the court if you need us," the younger of the two said. He knew the attorney would want them to be as unobtrusive as possible, but they had to weigh that with being responsible for the state's prisoner.

The knob to the door behind the justices' stand rattled. The person on the other side didn't know it was locked. Keys jangled and after a moment's hesitation the door opened. An armed officer serving as bailiff, entered and took his place standing at attention to the right and slightly rear of their desks to provide for the justice's security.

A moment later, they entered from the same door, behind their desks, and Wasserman and Pennington stood to acknowledge their presence.

The spokesman for the justices, the Chief Justice, Warren Murphy—a male in his early sixties, bald, except for a coating of silver on the sides and back of his shiny pate, with a silver beard—spoke.

Without reading from notes, Murphy said, "I'm sure you're aware, Mr. Wasserman, that the plaintiff doesn't have to speak," and displaying a hint of the attitude, for which he was known, added, "In fact, we'd rather he didn't, but we're a little on the informal side of things here so that's up to your discretion and you may do as you choose. And just to confirm, we're the court of record for convictions resulting from charges both here in Atlanta, and the ones in Chatham County. So, they're all our responsibility.

The bailiff, however, took his responsibility seriously, and clearing his throat to remind the chief justice they still had rules to follow, stepped forward and declared the hearing of the Appeals Commission of the great State of Georgia to be in session.

Chief Justice Murphy asked Wasserman, "Do you have any physical evidence to present on behalf of the plaintiff?"

"I do, Chief Justice." He picked up a sheaf of papers from the table surface and, thumbing through them, said, "This is a copy of psychiatric tests administered to Mr. Wentworth, and a copy of a report stating that in the opinion of the doctor, that the demon who committed the crimes is gone. I also have signed testimony from the warden of the Georgia Diagnostics and Classification Prison that Mr. Wentworth has been a model citizen since his return."

One of the assistants, a sober looking middle-aged man in a sober gray suit, approached the desk and collected the evidence from Wasserman, then respectfully approached the Chief Justice's aerie to pass it to him. Fortunately Pennington's attorney had the foresight to make seven copies. Musn't require additional work for the justices or their assistants.

Then he made his declaratory statement, describing the circumstance of Pennington's injury, the crimes for which he was convicted, stating that in his opinion, had he done a better job, the plaintiff wouldn't have been convicted and they wouldn't be in this position. He then continued to detail how the plaintiff had, according to sworn testimony by the respected psychiatrist, recovered from the brain injury and in fact, the entity that had committed the crimes no longer existed and Pennington deserved to have his conviction vacated.

Wasserman's opening statement took more than an hour and, upon the finish, Chief Justice Murphy said, "We'll take time to review the documents you've provided us and tomorrow morning at nine a.m. we'll return with questions, and I'm sure, to request additional information."

Wasserman stood and said, "Thank you, your Honor. We'll be prepared."

The justices stood and exited through the rear door.

The two officers returned for Pennington, and as they cuffed him, Wasserman said, "Well Pennington, no surprises here. I'm going back to the office and brush up on the information I anticipate them requesting."

"Yes, sir, Mr. Wasserman. I want you on top of your game. Call me if you need me. Oh, I forgot. You can't call me. I'm in prison."

"I'm glad you still have your sense of humor, Pennington, but hopefully be content you'll have reason to laugh and, soon."

"I hope so, sir."

***

"We've read the signed statements you've entered into the record, Mr. Wasserman," said the Chief Justice, "and we find the ones from both the psychiatrist, Dr. Kaplan, and his attending physician at Grady Memorial, Dr. Watters, particularly relevant. But we would like you to elaborate about the night Mr. Wentworth returned and the surrounding events."

"As it says in the record, your Honor, the night before Mr. Wentworth was to be executed, he went to the prison cafeteria to have his usual meal—that would be three hamburgers like he'd been eating three times a day for the previous three months. But once they were deposited on his tray, he looked at them and became sick to his stomach. It was at that moment he realized the entity know as 'Bad Penny' was gone."

One of the non-lawyer justices, cleared her throat, and when Chief Justice Murphy glanced her way, it was obvious she needed to discuss something with him.

"We'll take a fifteen minute recess," he said.

***

Once the justices returned, the Chief repeated verbatim Wasserman's testimony, then said, "So, Mr. Wasserman, you'd like the Supreme Court of the great State of Georgia to vacate Mr. Wentworth's eleven convictions of first degree murder and one of manslaughter, on the evidence of an upset stomach?"

One of the other justices covered her mouth in an attempt to stifle a chuckle at the statement's absurdity.

Wasserman stood and although he didn't say it with as much conviction as he would have liked, said, "With all due respect, Chief Justice Murphy, when taken as a part of the rest of the testimony I believe it to be not only relevant but it also paints a picture of a man who is *not* what he was."

It was now time for Pennington to clear his throat.

Wasserman glanced his way and Pennington raised his eyebrows. Wasserman's return glare could have blistered paint.

"Chief Justice, if it pleases the Commission, we'd like five minutes."

"Let's make it an hour and call it a break for lunch."

"Thank you, your Honor."

After the justices exited, Wasserman turned to Pennington. "What in the hell was so important that you had to interrupt me? *And* the proceedings?"

Meekly, Pennington said, "Forgive me Counselor, but I had the feeling...no, it's more than a feeling...it's like someone was telling me—no, commanding me to testify."

"Pennington, I can't allow—."

"With all due respect, sir, you work for me. And this is something I *must* do."

"Why, Pennington...for Christ's sake, tell me why?"

Pennington was pleading now. "It's like I said, Mr. Wasserman, I know it sounds crazy, but someone—or something—is whispering in my ears, commanding me to testify. And if I don't...well, there will be dire consequences."

"Don't tell me that, Pennington. It makes me question your stability. And that worries me. My reputation and your life are on the line here."

Attorney Ben Wasserman would have been really worried if Pennington had told him what else the Voice said. *That nothing that had happened to you or could happen to you in prison was as bad as whatever we will do to you if you aren't successful in freeing the both of you.*

"Mr. Wasserman—Ben, please. I beg you. I can handle it. I've got this." He felt sure that the Voice would help him say, and do, what he needed. Somehow, this Voice felt different than what he'd felt from his brain injury.

"Pennington, you heard what the Chief Justice said. They'd rather you not testify, although he didn't say you couldn't, but—and this is a *big but*—against my better judgement I will allow you to speak on your behalf. Should I hear anything that concerns me, however, I will cut you off immediately. Consider yourself warned. You are on a short leash. Do I make myself clear?"

"I understand, Counselor; but trust me, I can do this."

"I guess we'll find out, won't we? How about some lunch?"

"I could eat a salad, sir."

With the two uniformed officers as escorts, Wasserman and Pennington went to the first floor, where, with visitors in mind, the great State of Georgia had placed a coin- and credit card-operated refrigerated case containing various food items like one sees at the airport. Wasserman swiped his American Express Platinum Card and retrieved a chicken salad sub for himself and a salad with two hard-boiled egg halves for Pennington.

They returned to their table. "Thank you, sir," Pennington said when he accepted the meager salad. "I know I haven't had enough veggies since I was incarcerated in that terrible place."

"Well, from what you say, all you ate was beef."

"Yes. Can you believe it? Plus the occasional fish on Friday—thanks to the Catholics, God love 'em. And some chicken. Thank goodness they raise hens right on the prison grounds. So at least we had organic, free-range poultry. Yardbirds being raised by jailbirds." He slapped his knee and said, "I crack myself up."

"That was a good one, Pennington. Well, dig in. Enjoy. Hopefully you'll have a lot more salads when you get out, be able to eat what you want to again," Wasserman said.

"From your lips to God's ear, sir. *Buon appetito.*"

***

Upon returning from the lunch break, Wasserman told the court that, with its permission, Pennington wanted to speak on his own behalf.

A different justice cleared his throat and, with that, drew a hard stare of rebuke from the chief justice, who said, "As I mentioned earlier, it's not our typical way of conducting business, but we'll allow it."

Pennington began at the beginning. "I was a sensitive child. Even before I entered primary school a stern look could bring me to tears. More than once in school, comments from a teacher or other kids would cause me to go home sobbing over the most minor of reasons. And that brought my sainted mother to tears."

Pennington used a handkerchief to wipe the dampness from his eyes which seemed to appear on cue as he detailed pathetic memories. And then he apologized to the justices, saying he thought his days of weeping were behind him.

Wasserman had to admit that Pennington was doing an admirable job of telling his story. He only hoped that it was from the heart and not some deep, dark place that still existed—that maybe even Pennington himself didn't know was there.

After one of the justices asked for a short recess to confer, the

Chief asked Wasserman, "Counselor, we appreciate your client's life story, and his apparent sincerity, but we have to ask—specifically—just how relevant is this to the case and our decision?"

"Your Honor, with utmost respect, when you see the contrast between what my client was for most of his life, and then what he became, and what he has returned to now, we believe that the justices will have no choice—will be compelled, your honor— to overturn my client's convictions."

"All right, counselor, we'll give you and your client some leeway. But just make sure he doesn't stray too far from the mark."

"Yes, your honor. Consider him warned."

"Thank you, counselor."

Continuing his narrative, Pennington told of being bullied throughout his primary and secondary school years and how he couldn't find a girl to meet him at or go to the dances with him in middle school or high school and how he did his best to keep it from affecting him.

"I think we get the picture, Mr. Wentworth; so, would you please move closer to the series of events that brings us here?"

"Yes, Chief Justice…er, your honor, your eminence."

"Your honor is sufficient, Mr. Wentworth."

"Yes, sir, your honor, sir. Typically on weekends my friends and I would go to dinner, a comedy club, a dance club; I'm sure you know— or remember—how it is."

Pennington hadn't meant to insult the chief justice by implying he was old, but Wasserman felt like he needed to be careful with his choice of words. The attorney cleared his throat in an attempt to give Pennington a subtle warning.

It must have worked because Pennington looked Wasserman's way and gave him an impish wink which Wasserman concluded made Pennington look like someone he didn't recognize.

"So, moving along, your honors," Pennington said, deciding he shouldn't ignore the other justices, show them some respect—it couldn't hurt. "On the night in question, I and a few friends went to dinner, at Kyma—if you've been there, you know it's a lovely restaurant, wonderful seafood. I didn't eat meat, before my injury, because I've always been worried that eating meat would make one aggressive. Then we went to a comedy club, and followed that with dancing. By the time we decided to call it a night, it was raining.

"Anyway, I was returning home from midtown on the connector—you know how horrid the traffic can get any time of day, and it was too late to do anything about it—I saw there was a long traffic jam. And, for the longest time I couldn't remember any of this—until he was gone," Pennington assumed they'd know he meant Bad Penny. "But I hit my brakes, and in the rain and standing water, my cute little hybrid started to hydroplane and, oh this just breaks my heart, I slammed into the rear of one of those God-awful huge SUV things. I mean what are people thinking driving those? The *environment*…don't they care?

"Anyway, I slammed face-first into the windshield and was knocked unconscious sustaining a fractured skull. Two weeks later woke up in Grady—Grady Memorial, God bless them. I don't know where I'd be without Grady."

Again, Pennington gently wiped away his tears. "Although, I wasn't very kind to my doctor when I awoke. Which was just totally out of character from my norm."

The Chief Justice, visibly moved by this testimony, asked, "Can you please elaborate?"

"Of course, your honor. As soon as I awoke the doctor asked me if I remembered why, or knew anything about, what I was doing there. And it just pissed me off—oh, please forgive my language. I had never used that word before my brain injury, and I don't now, but I did at that time, so I'm just trying to keep it real."

"What else?" The Chief Justice asked.

"Well, he, the ER physician, explained what happened to me. The car accident, suffered a TBI, a traumatic brain injury, and that I could expect personality change, bouts of aggression, and changes in my likes and dislikes. Basically, he told me I would be a completely different person."

Pennington continued with his testimony the rest of the day and all of the next. He'd captivated the justices and it was evident they'd believed every word. The only thing that had bothered Wasserman was the occasional glance Pennington flicked his way, causing the barrister to imagine he saw a flash of Bad Penny in those charming eyes. And it also seemed that Pennington might have thought the story a fairy tale.

Upon Pennington's conclusion, the Chief Justice said, "Mr. Wasserman, we will have our decision by the end of day next Monday.

You may call my office for the result."

"Thank you, your honor. I will follow up with your office at close-of-business on Monday. Thank you again."

The justices exited, and before the police escorts made their way to collect Pennington, Wasserman said sotto voce, "Pennington, I believe with all my heart that they will vacate your conviction."

"From your lips to God's ear, sir."

"Pennington, I think after all we've been through together, you can call me Ben."

"I just want to be respectful, sir. But whatever you say, Ben."

***

Pennington entered Orpheus' Lair. "So tell me, young man, how did it go before the Conviction Appeals Commission?"

"Very well, Sensei. Ben, that's my attorney, Ben Wasserman; he's a very fine gentleman; he believes my conviction will be vacated and the chief justice said he'd have an answer for us by COB Monday."

"Fine, fine. We need to step up our studies then, if only three days more. First though, if you would be so kind, please recite for me the seven principles of the code of Bushido."

"I'm very happy to, Sensei." And Pennington recited the seven principles of Bushido.

Upon his completion, "Bravo, bravo," Orpheus exclaimed.

Finished with the study of the great philosophers, they moved to the study of history and particularly, because it was the Oracle's favorite time, and he thought it important in understanding the working of the U.S. Government, studying the Roman Empire and the all-important caesars.

"Dear boy, I'll start by saying that because there were over one hundred-seventy caesars, to be considered one of he greatest is no small accomplishment. History tells us the greatest Emperor of all time was the first, the man who founded the Roman Empire himself, the great nephew of Julius Caesar, Caesar Augustus. To honor him, the senate renamed the month, Sextilis, August, and being only thirty days originally, but not wanting the month to be subservient to July, named for his great uncle, Julius Caesar, they took a day from February and added it to August to make it the equivalent of July. Thus, February is so short. Many were his accomplishments. He led the building of a system of roads and highways unequaled at the time, connecting the nation states of the empire to Rome. Hence the saying, *All roads lead to Rome*."

"And although with today's modern technology, some might find this less important, but the postal system he created was vitally important to the people of the empire.

"Important to all writers, holders of liberal arts degrees and employees of universities offering such, he was a magnificent supporter of the arts and literature flourished during his reign. Splendid writers such as Horace and Virgil presented their unequalled works to the people of Rome during his time."

"And importantly, I believe, according to censuses, he grew the empire from barely over four million citizens to almost five million during his time. A growth rate of almost twenty percent. This was obviously done through expansion of the empire by increasing the number of nation states. But no other nation of comparable size has ever experienced such growth, since."

"Dear Orpheus, it sounds like he was a dynamic leader and just a lovely man. But it couldn't have been all good. What of his failures?"

"That's very prescient of you, young man. Caesar Augustus tried to make the people of Rome a more moral people, and at this he failed miserably. As well, he tried to incentivize the women of Rome to have more children, again, to grow the empire; this too was an abysmal failure. But, his greatest failure of all would have to have been on a personal and political level; he didn't set up a succession to the throne. This caused plots, infighting and murders. Other Caesars, if they didn't have a male scion to succeed them, adopted, and these kept the empire intact and kept it progressing and moving forward."

"Next, even though some might dispute me, in my humble opinion, would be Marcus Aurelius. His was a great intellect. A stoic philosopher, he led the empire to fight many battles and conquer many enemies. He did this all the while writing his famous Meditations; notes to himself and his ponderings on stoic philosophy. He was a great writer and philosopher and he fought and won many wars during his time. Caesar Aurelius was a moral leader with the utmost integrity. To anticipate your next question; his greatest failure was his son—specifically allowing his son, Commodus, to succeed him. The son's father, the esteemed Caesar, Marcus Aurelius, saw that he was highly educated but without a focus on military training. The father was consumed with the idea of having a bloodline son succeed him, due to the fact that he himself, like the previous four Caesars, had been adopted by their fathers and became leaders in that manner, so, he in fact made both Commodus and his older, twin brother, Caesars at the age of three. Their mother had been Faustina the Younger, Marcus Aurelius's first cousin, common in that time as it was, marrying first cousins; especially among royalty, being unwilling to mix with common blood. When Commodus' brother, Antonia, died at the age of four, Commodus became co-Caesar with the great Marcus Aurelius until the elder's death. He was the first emperor to be "born in the purple" meaning born of natural blood from his father. However, unlike his father, who was a highly moral man with immense integrity, Commodus was a corrupt ruler who believed himself the reincarnation of Hercules. He preferred a life of leisure and debauchery, drinking wine and having sex with whomever caught his eye, either female or male. In fact, he turned over the running of the empire to others so he wouldn't have to be involved in such mundane tasks and could pursue his…activities."

"As we continue, others are open to much debate, however my choice for the third greatest is Trajan. It was during his reign that the empire grew to its greatest boundaries. He was a great soldier-emperor who reigned over the empire's largest military expansion. In the 18th century the idea was put forth of the "Five Good Caesars." Trajan was number two. All new emperors after him were honored by the Senate with the wish "felicior Augusto, melior Traiano" which meant "be luckier than Augustus and better than Trajan".

"Alas, I tire of hearing my voice, young man, so unless you have any questions or there's anything you'd like to add to what I've said, why don't we call it a day?

"That's quite a lot for me to absorb, Orpheus, so why don't I retire to my quarters to review my notes and ponder your teachings."

"Splendid, my dear boy, splendid."

***

Breakfast was rice, potatoes and steamed vegetables. Not very tasty, but since Pennington had returned to his former food groups, and no longer ate meat, prison fare had become increasingly difficult for him to ingest.

He continued to dine with the Caucasian inmates with whom he'd grown comfortable. They asked and he told them that his hearing was going well.

Pennington's genteel manners had returned and taking longer than he had been to finish his meal, Joe, the first one he'd met, said, "So "Bad" see you at lunch." He'd taken to calling Pennington a shortened version of his self-bestowed sobriquet, "Bad" Penny.

"I think not, Joseph. God willing, I'll be released soon and I need to make sure I'm on top of my studies before I have to leave Orpheus."

As for keeping his head down and trying to stay alive until his hoped for release, it became increasingly easier to do. Word had gotten around that he was now under the watchful eye of Orpheus and no one wanted to go cross with Orpheus. And they especially didn't want to draw the ire of Gage.

***

Pennington kept as low a profile as possible all weekend. Just waiting to hear from his attorney at the end of day Monday, hopefully with good news. The news that would free him from this living worse than death he'd experienced for the last longer than half-year. He spent free time trying to decide how he'd kill himself if he wasn't released. Thinking all the while, how funny it was that he, an experienced killer, was having trouble trying to figure out how to end his own miserable existence. He only hoped it wouldn't come to that because he wouldn't be following the code of bushido.

***

Chief Justice Murphy arrived home Friday evening and being just Warren, husband, father and grandfather, brought up the garbage cans from the street before entering the door from the garage into the kitchen. Once inside, after the stress of the Wentworth hearing, he went to his favorite place in he house—the bar—and poured himself three fingers of Blanton's, hoping it would help him to sleep well, later. One of the finest bourbons in the world, Warren drank it neat, not even wanting ice cubes to dilute the sweet taste with its hint of citrus and oak. His wife, Donna had gone with her best friend for a manicure and massage and he turned in before she got home.

As it turned out, sleep was uneasy. He had nightmares he attributed to the stress of the hearing. Angry Voices told him he *must* vacate Wentworth's conviction or else his family—wife, children and grandchildren—were in grave danger. The Chief Justice couldn't remember when he'd last had a nightmare.

He welcomed daybreak as the nightmares would end once he woke.

He had planned lunch with his usual cohorts—he wouldn't call them partners in crime, since he was a judge, because of the appearance of impropriety— at Bobby Jones Golf Club, built in 1932 in tribute to one of the greatest golfers of all time, Bobby Jones, before they played eighteen holes. Like most male golfers over the age of fifty, he dreamed of playing on the Senior Tour, but being a ten handicap, when honest with himself, he knew there was little chance of that.

He'd promised his wife dinner and then Phantom Of The Opera at the Fox Theatre on Saturday night. They enjoyed an early dinner at Seasons 52 in Buckhead before leaving for the historic Fox.

Returning home, sleep was no better for Chief Justice Murphy. The Voice started again. This time he was told, "Free Wentworth. We don't care how you do it, as long as you don't tell the other justices. We choose our comrades carefully. If we'd wanted them to know, we would have gone to them." Murphy awoke about once every hour, drenched in sweat, but as cold as ice. It had to be a nightmare, but it felt real.

He was happy when the sun, announcing a beautiful Sunday, arrived. Sunday mornings were for mass at Cathedral Of Christ the King, Catholic church. Home to over one million Catholics in the Archdiocese of greater Atlanta.

After mass, lunch was at a small French bistro. Warren had a Mediterranean paella; Donna, a shrimp crepe with a small spinach salad. Each chose a fine French white burgundy.

After a good lunch and two glasses of fine wine, and returning home, Warren felt like having a nap. Turned on his huge HDTV to one of the last PGA tournaments of the season. He'd always joked that the golf announcers, with their soft-spoken commentary, could lull an insomniac to blissful sleep. Sitting on the end of a luxurious burgundy-colored leather sofa, he tilted back the section that became a recliner and dozed. But he didn't rest well. The Voice retuned, telling him he must overturn Wentworth's conviction.

He awoke, and the even stranger thing was that, even though awake, he was still hearing The Voice. He went to the master bedroom, and a bit freaked out, he went to the small safe he kept in the closet and withdrew the Glock 27, a .40, he kept for defense since he had sentenced some of Georgia's most violent criminals.

***

Five thirty p.m. Monday, and a guard spoke through Pennington's cell door: "Wake your sorry ass up and get to the interview room."

He was groggy from a nap. "Huh, what?" Trying not to think about his fate, he'd forced himself to sleep.

"Your attorney is here."

"Oh...really?"

"No, I'm lying. Get your sorry ass on deck. You don't want to keep him waiting. He's a gentleman."

Pennington groggily stumbled to his feet. Climbed into his pants and splashed some water on his face at the tiny stainless steel sink. His mind raced. *It must be good news or he would have called someone and had them tell me. But, maybe not. He would want to deliver bad news himself, after all we've been through together. Comfort me. Shit, I don't know.*

***

"Good evening Pennington." He had a smile on his face.

"Hello, Ben."

"I called the Chief Justice on my way over here, just so I could give you the news, good...or bad, in person. Fortunately for you, my friend, it's good news."

"You mean...?"

"Yes, you should be out of here by Wednesday. When the Great State of Georgia makes up its mind to correct an injustice it moves with speed and alacrity."

"I don't know what to say, except thank you." Pennington grasped Ben's hand to shake, and then pulled the surprised attorney in close to give him a hug. Ben had not received many hugs from grateful clients.

"You're very welcome, Pennington. Although I have to mention, they had a couple of conditions. You must see a psychiatrist every six months, just to make sure nothing strange is going on in that brain of yours. You must check in with me or my designee once a quarter. And you have to get involved in some kind of court-approved service— working with others, serving the community, etc. I have a list here of the types of things that are approved. They just want to try and keep you busy with something other than partying."

"Whatever they want, Ben. I'll do whatever they ask. No problem"

Chapter Five
Freedom

Ben sent a car for Pennington at 10:00 am Wednesday.

He'd changed from his prison stripes to the suit Ben had bought him for his trial. It wasn't the European cut fine fabric he was accustomed to, but it beat arriving at his tony high rise in prison black and white. That would bother most of his neighbors.

Walking through the lobby he was greeted by a new concierge, not that unusual as they usually got moved to different corporate-owned properties about once a year, showed his ID, and picked up a new key since his had long since disappeared, then passed two neighbors walking their dogs together, a white miniature poodle with an attitude, named Pearl, and a pretty chestnut-colored chihuahua with a ring of white around her nose, named Tinkerbelle, and squatted down to pet them. Once, he'd squatted, like now, to pet Pearl, she locked on to the tail of the expensive shirt he wore, with her sharp puppy teeth, and ripped it.

"Hey Tinker...,hey Tink, how's my girl?" as he patted her on her knotty head. He wanted to think she remembered him when she greeted him with wet doggy kisses, recognition in her chihuahua bugeyes. Tinker was a sweet dog who followed her owner around stuck to her like glue. The woman liked to dress her in different sweaters and outfits everyday and paint her toenails and carry her around in a Louis Vuitton purse. Tinkerbelle seemed embarrassed by it all.

***

Pennington's condo had been closed up for most of a year. But his friend, Ashley Denson, had asked her housekeeper to stop by to freshen it up for him when she heard on the local news he was being released. A Croatian woman, who said that Europeans were all good housekeepers but insisted that Croatians were the best, and she was best of them all.

The fragrance of Febreeze was fresh. Passing through the dining suite Pennington stepped into the glass-walled wine cellar, and withdrew a bottle of 2014 Caymus Cabernet Sauvignon from a wooden crate, and poured a glass of the now extra-aged wine and headed straight to his terrace. The bottle was the last one from a case he'd bought at the Caymus winery on his last trip to Napa Valley. Plopped into one of the two teak chaise lounge chairs to gaze at the view of the north Georgia mountains he'd missed while incarcerated. Turning thoughtful: *I ought to go hiking in the mountains, see them up close sometime. Who am I kidding? I'd rather sit here with a glass of wine and just say I did.* He held the glass up to the light of the sky, tilted it and examined the color. He loved the opulent red and could taste the vibrant dark cherry and blackberry layered with subtle warm notes of vanilla.

Pennington watched the thousands of cars passing on the roadway below and studied God's creations—the mountains and trees, and sky. It was times like this when he understood how small and unimportant he was.

Late August and in another month, the mountains would be ablaze with the colors of autumn. Reds, oranges, yellows and purples. Pennington loved the autumn season and If he'd known how good the north Georgia wineries were he'd probably make a day trip to the mountains even though he didn't hike.

***

Pennington spent a few days getting settled. Had to to get his fall clothes moved to the front of his walk-in closet and the summer ones moved to the rear. He found out that some of his wardrobe basics no longer fit from his months of working out and the resultant muscle gains. He'd have to go to his favorite mens' stores, the high end boutiques at Lenox Square Mall to pick out some new additions to his wardrobe. Checked on his investments. Then called Ashley to see if she wanted to have dinner with him at Il Giallo. A new restaurant near his condo, he'd heard his neighbors talking about it and according to them, had an excellent wine list and European fusion food to die for. Sounded like his kind of place.

***

Pennington, once again the complete gentleman, asked Ashley to meet him at the classic new restaurant at seven on Saturday night, and driving the new Toyota Prius hybrid he'd bought to replace the one that was destroyed in the accident, he arrived at 6:45 so she wouldn't wonder if he was there.

"Pennington, it's so good to see you." And in the way of Europeans she kissed him on both cheeks

"You, too, luv. You look beautiful as usual."

"Thank you. And you look awesome, Pennington. In great shape." Even Ashley noticed the change in his body with the muscles he'd built while in the Bad Penny incarnation.

A painting of Bacchus the Roman God of food and wine hung over the bar. Once seated Pennington ordered a bottle of Far Niente Chardonnay and immediately directed the conversation toward Ashley by asking about her work, her friends, and acquaintances and her family since all he would be able to talk about was prison and that wouldn't be pleasant for either of them.

The sommelier, who was also the general manager and one of the two owners of the restaurant, personally brought over the Far Niente and placed it in a tableside stainless steel chiller.

Using a corkscrew, the sommelier de-corked the bottle and offered Pennington a taste, him deferring to his guest, however.

Ashley swirled a mouthful. "That's delightful."

"Excellent. I'm glad you like it," Pennington gushed.

She coyly dipped her head without replying.

A moment later the server took their orders.

"So, how are things?" Pennington missed his previous life and was anxious to get involved with his former friends. He hoped they wouldn't treat him any differently. He was back in his element.

Ashley decided to get what was for her, the elephant in the room, out in the open.

"Pennington, I hope you can forgive me for the things I said at your trial. We've been friends for almost twenty years. I'm so sorry." She'd wanted to get this off her chest for awhile. "You know me almost better than almost anyone. You know I can't lie."

"Ash, think nothing of it. It's over and done. I'm out now. I'm resuming my life and going to pick up where I left off—before him— (he still had a difficult time referring to that part of himself as "Bad Penny") and not look back. I want to get back to my charity work. Give back, you know. Just get back to living by helping others. And you and

I have been friends too long. Nothing will ever change that."

" 'Ash'—you haven't called me that in so long. I've missed it."

"Well, I've missed calling you 'Ash.' Of course, I've missed calling you anything."

"You're so sweet. It sounds like the old Pennington is back. The old Pennington I remember, and care so deeply for."

"You don't have to worry about that, Ash. He's back."

The server returned with an appetizer they shared, a dish of spicy Asian-style calamari.

After trying a small piece, "Oh my goodness. This calamari is to die for," said Ashley. "It's much more tender than most restaurants have."

"Certainly better than anything I've eaten lately." The fine food was a reminder of the wretched prison food.

"I'm sorry, Pennington. I shouldn't have said anything."

"It's not a problem, Ashley. Don't worry yourself."

They finished the calamari in silence, Ashley afraid she would say something thoughtless and Pennington, unable due to his time in lockup to indulge in idle conversation.

The server brought their dishes, Pennington, returning to his vegetarian diet, had the tortelli pasta filled with butternut squash and shiitake mushrooms and Ashley, the agnello; lamb shank braised with red wine.

"This looks just beautiful, Pennington."

"It sure does."

"So, what do you have planned?"

"Get back to normal as quickly as possible. In fact I need to call my dentist's office first thing in the morning—get an appointment with my hygienist. Prison dental care is the worst. They absolutely kill you."

"That had to be terrible for you, Pennington. I know how meticulous you've always been about taking care of your mouth."

"It'll be fine. I'll call in the morning."

They asked their server to take pictures with Ashley's iPhone before leaving.

"I'm going to have to get a new iPhone. They've improved dramatically since I've been... away."

***

"Good morning, Dr. George's office." In an attempt to comfort patients from their first contact, the receptionist answered in a soothing tone.

"Good morning, this is Pennington Wentworth, II. I'd like to make an appointment with Lisa Holley for a cleaning."

"I'm sorry, Mr. Wentworth, Lisa is no longer with us. I can give you an appointment with Andrea Milton, however.

"I'm sure sorry to hear that, but I'll take it." He figured anyone they would have would be better than any prison hygienist hired by the government.

Pennington sat in the lobby reading entertainment news on his iPad, happy to have it and internet access again.

The door opened to the back of the office and an attractive woman in her mid-thirties with light brown hair said, "Hi, I'm Andrea."

Pennington rose and extending his hand, said, "Pennington, nice to meet you."

As they walked to her small exam room, "I have your records and you seem to be in good shape, but since it's been over a year since we've seen you we should probably take some pictures. Then set you up on a regular schedule."

"Whatever you say, darling."

They moved to the rear most room and he stepped into the x-ray machine, and, placed his chin on the small rest. The machine began to whir around him.

"Now, don't move."

After the device stopped spinning, she said, "Okay, you can step out now."

He returned to her small office and sat in the examination chair and said, "Lisa cleaned my teeth since I was a teenager, probably close to twenty years. It's pretty stressful breaking in a new hygienist, let alone having someone new look in my mouth."

"I'll be gentle, and believe me, I've seen far worse than anything that might be wrong with you. And I don't judge."

"I hope not." *'Cause I'd hate to have to kill you and break in another new hygienist. That would be additional stress I don't need.'*

Pennington was stunned by himself. He couldn't believe he'd thought that. It sounded like something Bad Penny would say, which worried him much more than someone new peering into his mouth.

A picture on the wall showed Andrea with a young man. "Is that your husband?"

" His name is Carl."

"Nice looking guy. How'd you meet?"

"He teaches CPR and as a dental hygienist I have to be qualified so I met him in a class he was teaching."

"That's cool. Kind of like a girl falling in love with her sexy Latin dance instructor."

"I don't know about that. But it worked for us." She was a little off put by his inappropriate comment.

Close to finishing she asked, "What flavor toothpaste would you like? Grape, bubble gum, or cinnamon?"

"I'm a cinnamon guy, and if you don't use it I might as well use Fireball cinnamon-flavored liqeur as mouthwash."

"Don't worry. I'll use it."

"And I'm sure you'll remember so you'll never have to ask again."

"You know, since I was away and unable to get good dental care I think I'd like to start getting cleanings four times a year. At least until we know I'm good."

"You can do that. But you are aware insurance will only pay for twice a year.

"That's okay. I'd rather keep my teeth."

"Let's set up the next one, then. Ninety days out."

Feeling good about having clean teeth without being hurt, one of the first steps in returning to normal, Pennington set about to returning to his former life. With the help of Ashley's housekeeper, and with a clean condo, he decided he must have a cocktail party.

***

Pennington had to find where he'd written down Ashley's phone number. Once finding it he touched "CREATE A NEW CONTACT" in his iPhone so he'd have it.

She answered and he didn't say hello. "Ash, I want to have a cocktail party, and I need a female co-host. What do you think? You up for it?"

"Pennington, you didn't even have to ask. You know you can count on me. When do you want to have it?"

"A week from Saturday?"

"I could do that, but you know how the autumn party season is in Atlanta. This is still the old money south. People get booked early. The next Saturday might be better."

"Okay, then let's do it. You know I can't do it without you. And I also need your list of email addys and phone numbers since I lost most of mine." He couldn't tell her that Bad Penny had thrown his previous iPhone in a creek so he wouldn't have to talk to any of those same people that he now wanted to invite to a party that would herald his return to genteel society.

"I'll text you the names with numbers and emails."

"But we'll need to do this fast or everyone will have plans."

"I'll get them to you before I go to bed."

"Thanks, Ash. You're the best."

***

Upon checking out the names and numbers Ashley had sent him, Pennington put faces and memories —some good, some not so good— with the names.

He decided to first call the ones with the numbers and knowing most people wouldn't recognize his number and would screen their calls, left a string of voice mails. He gave Ashley's name and number to RSVP. He then sent emails to the rest. It took the whole morning to finish the list.

Pennington decided to skip a day before following up.

"Hey, darling," he said to Ashley when she answered. "What do you think?"

"I honestly don't know, Pennington. I've received about twenty positive responses, but that doesn't mean they'll all show, just like it doesn't mean the ones who haven't responded, won't.

"Okay, so what do we do?"

"Nothing. We've extended invitations. Now, we wait...and hope."

***

Because there was a gym in the lobby of Pennington's building, he could continue working out just like he were in prison, but in a much more pleasant environment. Accustomed to early starts in the joint, he rose at six a.m. and went downstairs to get his first workout as a free man.

One of the latino handymen in the building was wiping down workout equipment when he entered.

Trying to channel some of the machismo he acquired in prison, he said, "Dude," to the worker, remembering how macho the latinos had been in the joint.

As an employee of the building management company however, and expected to be deferential to condo owners, he said, quietly and respectfully, almost with a bow, "Good morning, sir."

Oh my, Pennington thought, *things aren't the same on the outside as they are on the inside.*

He warmed up by knocking out a set of fifty pushups. Then, with his shoulders properly pumped with blood, he moved to the bench press machine, put the pin on one-hundred-fifty-five pounds and got twelve reps. Moved the pin to one-hundred-eighty-five and pumped out ten.

Raised the poundage once more, setting it on two-hundred-five pounds, but managed only three reps. Not bad, but It seemed since ending his sessions with Orpheus his strength was suffering as well.

He finished with machine shoulder presses and then did a set of dips on the stand bolted onto the shoulder press machine.

His workout over, Pennington showered and decided he needed to replace some of the personal grooming products he'd lost track of during his time away. Went to a local Target Store and bought a high end Sonicare dental appliance, a rotary trimmer to clip nose and ear hairs and several bottles of Old Spice shower gel. Pennington obsessed about dental hygiene and he was worried about it since his time with prison dentists. Without a trimmer in prison to clip errant hairs he thought he'd looked like a hairy wild weasel. And soap in prison was the worst. His skin stayed dry, and he couldn't have it even one day longer.

And he just had to have a new coffee maker. He hadn't had good coffee in so long—prison coffee sucked—he couldn't wait to get a new high end Cuisinart grinder/maker to run his favorite fresh Starbucks' beans through every morning. His next stop after Target was his local branch of Wells-Fargo, where he got a cashiers check for nine-hundred thousand dollars to send to Orpheus' wife.

Mission accomplished, Pennington returned to his condo and in the middle of the afternoon, took his second shower of the day so he could use his new shower gel, shaving under the spray with his new, best-in-the-world, German-made stainless steel razor blades. After the shower, applying the three different skin creams he bought, one for wet skin and two different ones for dry skin, one for the surface and one a deeper use cream, to try and rid himself of the parchment-like epidermis he'd developed while in prison and also using the rotary trimmer to eradicate the wild nose and ear hairs that had been driving him crazy for months. He brushed his teeth, gums, roof of his mouth and the insides of his cheeks with the same care he'd always taken, using the new high speed dental appliance. Then used his cinnamon-flavored floss for the first time in months. It had been difficult to practice proper hygiene while incarcerated. He only hoped it hadn't caused irreparable long term harm to his teeth and gums.

Admiring himself before the full-length mirror in the shower he was pleased with the result. Clean shaved, brushed, flossed, conditioned skin, smelling sweet and rid of unwanted hair growing in atypical places.

"Damn, I look…and feel good." He surprised himself by swearing. He hadn't done that since Bad Penny exited his body, mind and soul.

Deciding he looked so good he needed to share it with the women of Atlanta, he called his best friend.

On the phone; "Ash, you want to hit the floor tonight? I don't know which floor. Your call. I've been gone too long. But I feel like dancing."

"That sounds good, Pennington."

"Great. Shall I pick you up?'

"If you don't mind. Nine-ish?

"Mind? Please, Ash. I don't mind at all. I'll be in your lobby at nine."

"Thank you, Pennington, but remember, I can't stay out too late. I have to work in the morning."

"I remember. We don't have to stay late."

***

The elevator opened and Ashley exited, stylishly dressed in the latest fashion and accessories from Saks 5th Avenue. She air-kissed

Pennington on each cheek.

"You look beautiful, Ash."

"You don't look so bad yourself. And you smell great."

"Thanks, darling." He was wearing Vanille Tobacco, by Tom Ford, a rich and spicy new fragrance that hit the stores while he was incarcerated.

"Of course I'm glad the long sleeves cover up the tattoos. Fortunately I only got them on my arms."

What was I thinking? But it wasn't him thinking. Bad Penny had gotten the tats. He only wished he and Bad Penny hadn't been the same person, even temporarily.

"So," he asked, "where are we going?".

"Tongue & Groove is still the best place in town."

"I probably shouldn't go back there, Ash." He left the reason hanging on the dead air; that Bad Penny had picked up one of his victims at the oldest dance club in Atlanta before killing her, and was afraid it could turn into an ugly scene if anyone recognized him. And the bartender who'd served him that night had testified against him. And although he didn't hold it against the man, he thought it best not to risk it. And most bartenders at the better bars and clubs in the ATL considered it a proud profession and tended to stay in those positions for years, so since it had only been some months, it was almost guaranteed he would still be there.

"What about Reign," he asked, "is it still a good place?"

"It closed. Sorry" Ashley said hesitatingly,

"That sucks."

"How about Opera Atlanta?"

"That's cool. Wherever you think."

"Okay, then. That's it."

"Good. It's settled, then."

It was just a few minutes to Opera Atlanta's Peachtree Road midtown location. Peachtree was the spinal cord, the lifeblood, of Atlanta, especially at night. As important to the ATL as Broadway to New York City, or the strip to Las Vegas.

***

Pennington dropped off Ashley at the entrance and went to park the car in a lot. By the time he returned she was third in line behind a young couple. It was a surprisingly short wait to get in on a Thursday night. They settled into a comfortable booth, the club both dark and flashy with neon lights. Pennington ordered his new preferred drink from about the time he morphed into Bad Penny—a Macallan 12. Ashley ordered a lemon drop martini.

"They make the best lemondrops here."

"And their Macallan is too die for," Trying to be funny since it's the same everywhere.

"You know I don't remember you drinking scotch before."

"I didn't. I developed a taste for it after my TBI. And I still like it. The smokey taste reminds me of different flavors of wine."

"I see, " she didn't want to dwell on that period of time, "by the way, did I ever tell you about the time my niece, Gracie—you'd love her, she's a doll—was about three, someone asked her if she wanted to have kids when she was older, and when she answered 'Yes', then the lady asked her how many, Gracie said, three, one of each. I think she was talking about a boy, a girl and a dog."

Pennington, leaning back in his seat, roared. "That's the funniest thing I've ever heard."

"Isn't it though?"

Then, downing the drink in one continuous gulp, he said, "Let's hit the floor."

"Okay."

Pennington and Ashley danced to a couple of songs and after returning to their booth, emboldened by his dress and his moves, Pennington said, "If you don't mind I'm going to make a loop of the club, see if there are any women I want to dance with."

"Of course I don't mind, Pennington. I know this is a treat for you. I'll be here when you get back."

Excusing himself and rising, after smoothing his lapels and giving his package a tug, he put on his coolest gait and most insouciant attitude to make a lap around the club.

Some of the women checked out Pennington. It seemed that the little swagger that still remained from Bad Penny's adventures and time in prison attracted a certain type of woman. But it also pissed off the men they were with or the ones that wanted to be with them, or at least the expressions on their faces sent that message to Pennington.

"Would you care to dance?" he asked of a pretty blonde girl who politely declined. He thought it the kindest rejection he'd ever received.

"Thank you, anyway, my love. I appreciate the consideration."

Returning to the booth where Ashley sat, he said, "Hey Ash, I hope you don't mind, but this place is boring me to tears. How about we have another round and then take our leave?"

"Whatever you like, Pennington. I just came because you wanted to."

"Alrighty, then." And with that he waved at the server to flag her down and ordered two more.

"Another Macallan 12?" She asked,

"No, that 12-year-old isn't even old enough to vote. Make it the 18 this time."

When finished with their cocktails, Pennington pulled out his American Express and looking at it wistfully, "I don't know what I would have done without Ben. My attorney? When I didn't have any memory of who I was I threw out this card and didn't pay any bills because I didn't even know where I lived to pick up mail. But after I was arrested and incarcerated, I gave Ben control of my assets and he took care of paying my bills for me, thank the Lord. And fortunately for me, Amex was very forgiving."

"Well, thank you again, for treating, Pennington."

"Believe me, Ash. It's my pleasure."

Ashley was happy to see that Pennington seemed truly back to his previous self.

Back in the car, Pennington said, "Yeah, Ash, I don't know what it is, but as much as I wanted to return to this life, after he left and I remembered who I was, tonight it just seems so unfulfilling and I want—no, need—more"

"Wow. I'm impressed. That's very mature of you, Pennington."

"Don't you think it's about time?" He continued to be ashamed of not only his time inhabited by "Bad Penny," but his libertine lifestyle before then, and he had hopes of atoning for both.

"Don't be so hard on yourself, Pennington. We know it wasn't you and you need to quit blaming yourself for it."

"You're giving me too much of a break, Ash."

"You need to give yourself a break. You've been exonerated. It wasn't you."

"And Ash, to tell you the truth, I miss my sensei, Orpheus—he's my mentor—something terrible. When I was studying the great philosophers and martial arts, I was just so focused, had clarity of thought, like never before. And even though Bad Penny had already disappeared I credit Sensei for the turnaround that I feel confident is going to be permanent."

"I'm sure you're right, Pennington."

Chapter Six
Return to Normalcy

Saturday afternoon and Ashley showed up at Pennington's mid-afternoon just to make sure things were in order.

Seeing the large armful of flowers she carried, he said, "Ashley, you shouldn't have."

"I know my housekeeper brought flowers, but that was last week. We needed fresh ones for tonight."

"Well, I can't argue with that. You know how I like fresh flowers."

"I know, dear, and besides, I used your American Express. I still have the number."

"Okay, that's okay, then."

"Where are your vases?'

"There are three or four in the pantry." Pennington poured two glasses of wine.

Ashley busied herself dividing the array of flowers into smaller bouquets, placing them in the vases on the dining-room table, the living-room coffee table and on tables on each end of the sofa. She then set up her iPad to attach to a blue-tooth speaker she bought for music. Pennington watched her and she said, "I assumed you don't have any current music so I brought mine on my iPad. And I used your card to buy you this speaker."

"Thanks, Ash. That was good thinking and sweet of you."

"I just figured you could use it."

"You figured right."

Fortunately Pennington liked Ashley's taste in music. It was similar to his own and he knew it would be good for a party. As '24k Magic,' the new album by Bruno Mars, started to play, he handed her a glass and when she looked at him doubtfully, he said, "It's five o'clock somewhere."

"Same old Pennington."

"Thank God." She understood the connotation. "Cheers."

"Cheers."

He gestured to the French doors off the living room. "You want to go out on the terrace for awhile before the guests arrive? The fall temps are nearly perfect and the trees are beginning to change."

Let's. I'm sure it will be lovely."

"What a pretty planting," she said as they stepped outside. "What is that? A blue spruce?

" Technically a dwarf blue spruce, but thanks, Ash. I picked them up at the nursery yesterday. They grow like crazy in our chilly north Georgia fall and winter. If I can remember to keep them watered. I don't exactly have a green thumb." He'd centered the small tree most people thought of as a Christmas tree in the center of three purple cabbages in a large terra cotta pot he'd bought at his local yard and garden center. Growing to about six feet he already planned to decorate it with colored lights for the holidays and thought it would make a Christmassy addition to his terrace when lighted up at night.

Lying on their backs in the twin chaises, they gazed at the brilliant blue autumn sky and watched and listened as airliners from both U.S. and international metropolises entered the airspace of the world's busiest airport. The gleeful sounds of kids playing soccer on the artificial turf field in the city park in the next block to the west were audible on his twenty-fourth floor.

But Pennington thought about the planes. "You know, Ash, when I was a kid I used to watch jets fly over, wondering where they were going, or coming from, and wish I were on one. Going to exotic places. Then when I was in middle school father took us on a summer vacation to Europe—Spain, Italy and France—it was a great experience for a young kid, and it taught me an important life lesson at an early age; that people are basically the same everywhere. Except for the language differences, of course. It was an incredible trip, but foreign countries kind of lost some of their appeal for me after that. I'd rather stay in the good old US of A."

***

At eight o'clock the doorbell rang, not for the last time.

Two couples, all friends, planning ahead, had rendezvoused in the lobby and stepped into the elevator for the little over a minute-long ride to Pennington's penthouse.

"Brook, Warner, so good to see you." Pennington had to search the recesses of his mind for their names.

"It's lovely to see you, Pennington, and you too, Ashley." Brook said, "And of course you remember Sophie and Gentry."

"Of course I do." He turned to Ashley and said, "Ash, say hello to Sophie and Gentry. Looking very on fleek, Gentry."

"Pennington, don't leave your guests standing in the hallway. Come in." Pennington, in sotto voce, said to Ashley, "Be sure and say someone's names when you greet them just in case I don't remember them."

"Yes, come in, come in. Would you like some wine?"

Pennington had gone to his local wine superstore that morning and stocked up. Bottles of riesling, chardonnays and an assortment of reds.

For the next thirty minutes guests continued to arrive as singles and in pairs. The women stylishly dressed in the latest fall fashions from Nordstrom's, Saks 5th Avenue, Neiman Marcus and other fashion forward stores. The men not quite as fashionable, but looking classic and comfortable in Polo slacks, dress shirts and sweaters or sport coats for the cool weather of early autumn. All with fresh expensive hairdos, haircuts and manicures. Pennington was thrilled with the quality of the people compared to the types he'd been associating with in prison for many months. Most of all he was happy to be back among them.

A cute little brunette, Courtnee, arrived unescorted. Her hair was the color of dark chocolate with caramel streaks.

Ashley made the introduction.

"Pennington, I'd like you to meet my friend, Courtnee Shows. We work together."

"It's lovely to meet you, Courtnee," and then to Ashley, "Where have you been hiding this one?"

"Like I said, we work together."

"It's very nice to meet you, Pennington. Thank you for allowing me to come."

"Your place looks great, Pennington." Lace and her fiancée Talon, had been there before, but it had been quite awhile. Of course no one had been there in quite awhile, including Pennington.

"Thank you, but I can't take any credit, luv. It's all thanks to Ash's housekeeper, Mirka, she's from Hranice, Czech Republic and she's wonderful. And of course Ash's touch with the flowers."

"Oh, can I get her number, Ashley? I could use a new housekeeper."

"I'll give it to you before you leave. But you'll have to call her soon. She just told me she's pregnant and she's going to stop taking on any new clients until after the baby comes. Her husband is a Spaniard and they're both so cute they make beautiful babies. Sometimes she brings her eldest daughter with her to help. She can make up a bed better than I can and she's only nine. Mirka pays her out of what I give her. She says she's saving up for a laptop. This will be their fourth child. They're Catholic, you know. Three girls and the new baby is a boy. She says her husband, Marcelo, is so excited he beams all the time."

"By the way, you all are welcome to step out on the terrace. The mountains to the north are fairly dark except for a few lights from homes, but you can see the lights and make out the buildings of perimeter north." Pennington enjoyed the cool fresh autumn air at that height and thought his guests would like it, too.

Though he wasn't a fan, he turned it on for the other guys and the last quarter of the Georgia football game, with the sound off, was counting down on the large screen tv on the living room wall.

Three couples wandered out to the terrace where two chaise lounges along with a glass-topped bistro table and two tall chairs provided seating for them all. Pennington made sure they were comfortable.

Most of the others gathered around the dark mahogany contemporary dining table which had an unusual feature—shallow drawers underneath the top running the length of each side—on top of which an array of dishes from Pennington's colorful Gail Pittman collection, holding beautiful seasonal foods, were displayed. The wine fridge in the end of the kitchen island was also a popular spot for gathering.

Warner, Pennington and Gentry returned from the terrace a few minutes later and Gentry, excited, like he had the best idea ever, said, "Pennington! We think you should have a Fourth of July party. All the fireworks displays in the area would have to be spectacular from up here."

A cover of *Queen's Bohemian Rhapsody* by *Panic At The Disco* played from Ahley's iPad hidden. It was followed by their mega hit, *The Death of a Bachelor*.

"It is fairly awesome. Maybe I'll do that next year. Of course, New Year's Eve is pretty great, too," Pennington said, glancing at the date on his watch. "And it's only two months away. And if there happens to be snow the moon gives a blue tint to every surface and flashes from the fireworks shining off the icy white ground are spectacular."

Warner said, "It's settled, then. New Year's Eve party at Pennington's place to watch the fireworks." He sounded like a high school kid planning a party when the parents were away.

Pennington, always ready with a clever retort, replied, "I'm glad we didn't waste any time making a decision."

Fallout Boy was singing about someone wanting to dance like Uma Thurman.

Pennington turned to Ashley. "So, you ready to do this again New Year's Eve?"

''Why not?" And shrugged her shoulders. She didn't sound excited about it but didn't say no.

Then, the women moved to the kitchen to open more wine and the guys returned to the terrace. Still remembering it as something Bad Penny would like, Pennington brought out a box of expensive Cuban cigars.

Ashley noticed what he was doing."I can't say anything because we're not a couple and besides, it's his place so he can smell it up if he wants to, but I hate cigar smoke."

"It is disgusting, isn't it?" Agreed Sophie, "Whenever Gentry has his buddies over they have to light up those damn things. By the way, Ashley, how's Pennington holding up?"

"I think he's doing okay, but we don't talk about it that much."

On the terrace, between puffs on a cigar, Warner said, "So, Pennington, how are you doing?"

"I'm fine."

"No. I mean with the elephant in the room—I mean, considering the months in prison, how *are* you?"

The Angel of Small Death And The Codeine Scene by *Hozier* played over the outdoor speakers.

"I like that song. Anything that glorifies death."
I don't care what you like.

Gentry gave Warner a look that could have killed. He couldn't believe he'd bring that up. Of course he figured that some of the people came to the party *because* he's a serial killer. He'd heard of the phenomenon of"Serial Killer Chic" before. He just didn't thinkWarner would have been one of them.

"Oh, that. I'm okay. It's different, you know. Being able to do anything I want to, any time I want to, eat good food, drink good wine and live in three thousand square feet instead of a ten foot by eight foot cell, I mean, all in all, life is good."

"Well, all that's good, but did you really do it?"

Pennington was going to make him work for it. "Do what?"

"You know what—kill all those people."

Pennington remained obtuse, "Technically, yes, but if you've read any newspaper in the Great State of Georgia, you know I was freed because the verdicts at trial were overturned due to the Conviction Appeal Commission being convinced that I didn't know what I was doing, because of my goddamn fractured skull."

"How did it feel?"

"To kill someone?"

I can't believe this son of a bitch had the guts to say that to my face. Bad Penny would throw him off the fuckin' balcony. Well, he asked for it. So he's going to get it.

"It depends is the answer. When you cut someone's throat, it's just kind of bloody and warm when you get the backwash on your hand and lower arm. But when I killed the Monsignor by caving in his skull with the gold chalice; The first blow is just like hitting a coconut with a ball peen hammer, but then, after it crushes his skull, all the following blows are going into the brain and it gets all soft and squishy and when you pull the hammer out of his brain it sounds like pulling a boot free when it's stuck in mud. And when it comes free you can see gray chunks of brain and huge amounts of blood flying around. It's pretty cool."

You could see looks of fascination on a couple of faces and astonishment and disgust on a couple others.

Turning a yellow shade of green Warner looked like he was going to be sick.

Pennington said, "Excuse me," and hurriedly scampered to the master bath where he promptly threw up. *That was harder than I thought it would be.* Seeing his reflection in the mirror churned his stomach. For a moment he thought he glanced the hardened visage of Bad Penny in the mirror.

"Yes, it's me, and it was US that did it."

In the kitchen, Courtnee quietly said to Ashley, "So, you and Pennington are just friends?"

"Definitely, Courtnee, why do you ask?"

"Well," blushing, she said, "I think he's kind of cute."

Ashley looked at her with a knowing grin. "Then my devious plan is working."

Still blushing, Courtnee said, "So you'll give him my number?"

"Only if you really want me to."

Warner, still looking sickly from Pennington's murderous recitation, wandered in, and taking Brook by the hand, said to the small group of women, "I hate to be a pooper, but we should probably be on our way."

Brook gave him a light swat on the shoulder and said, "Oh, you, you know you like being a pooper."

He inclined his head, knowing he didn't look sincere. Gave her a sweet wan smile and said, "Guilty."

Brook and Warner's departure started an exodus.

Goodnights were exchanged. Promises to get together, soon. As always, some would happen, some wouldn't.

Courtnee made the decision to linger until the others had left.

After seeing everyone out, Pennington turned to her and said, "How much wine have you had?" He didn't want anything to happen to her on his watch.

"Not that much. Only two glasses."

"That's good, but how about a cup of coffee just to be on the safe side?"

"Sounds good."

"Ashley," he said across the room as she fluffed sofa pillows, "would you care for a cup of coffee?"

"Sure, I'll have one."

He pulled his Keurig coffee maker from the low shelf where he kept it so they could each choose what they wanted from the small sealed plastic cups of various flavors.

"What kind would you like?"

"Do you have a macchiato?"

"Sure do. Ash, how about you?"

"French Vanilla?"

"Coming up. And the host will have a peppermint latte'."

Pennington pulled out three Starbucks mugs of various colors and styles he'd collected through the years, poured the coffees and placed them on a tray. "I usually buy a Starbucks mug whenever I travel. Different cities or especially countries will have a cup with a local site or important landmark on it."

"That sure makes for an interesting memento," Courtnee said.

"Why don't we retire to the living room?"

"Sounds good."

Pennington and Courtnee lowered themselves onto the leather sofa set at a ninety degree angle to a matching loveseat. The sofa faced the wide screen tv sitting in an entertainment center custom-made from rusticated, reclaimed Georgia barn wood, centered on the exposed brick wall, its flanking shelves filled with the types of novels Pennington enjoyed reading. Most of them chick-lit with some historical fiction current to the period before Bad Penny went on his killing spree, then to prison, the chick-lit far outnumbering the historical fiction.

The grayish-brown stained, gnarly grain of Georgia pine clearly visible, it, along with the brick wall and ancient brown oriental rug with pastel blue flowers resembling a fringed flying carpet, on which the coffee table sat, were the only pieces of furniture or accessories that weren't modern. He felt the handmade piece connected him to the proud pre-Revolutionary War history of his home state. The coffered ceiling was originally constructed of rich, shiny dark mahogany, but he'd had the massive beams replaced with ones made of reclaimed barn wood to match the other barn wood pieces. The short sofa Pennington referred to as the loveseat faced a wall of books, many signed first editions.

Hearing the soft sound of a toilet flushing next door made them realize just how quiet it had become since everyone had left.

Once seated on the loveseat, coffee in one hand, Ashley leaned forward and rearranged the flowers on the coffee table with the other. Making sure they were perfectly spaced and the different autumn colors—orange, yellow and red—symmetrically positioned. Then she shifted the coffee table about an inch on one end. It had apparently been bumped earlier, with all the people in the room.

"Ashley, relax. You're off the clock now."

"Oh, Pennington. I don't want you to have to spend your Sunday cleaning house."

"Well, thank you, Ash, but that's not your responsibility." And to his guest, he said, "Have you had a nice time, Courtnee?"

"Very nice, Pennington. Thank you. And this macchiato sure is good."

"Yeah, there were some real nice people here." He thought he'd give Warner a break for his rude behavior. And he ignored her compliment on the coffee. He thought it passable at best. Once you've had the real thing the flavored cups just wouldn't do. Of course he had to admit it was way better than prison coffee.

"Yes there were." Courtnee glanced at Ashley and knowing her friend could read between the lines, her faced flushed to a vivid shade of pink. She hoped Pennington wouldn't know she was referring to him.

Noticing that she had finished her coffee, he said to her "Why don't I see you to your car, or at least to the valet stand."

"That would be nice, Pennington. If it's not too much trouble."

"No trouble at all."

Ashley was returning untouched food to Pennington's huge Viking refrigerator and returning unopened bottles of wine to the glass-enclosed wine cellar.

Pennington retrieved Courtnee's coat, and using it to gesture with toward the door, asked, "Are you ready?"

Still somewhat shy, Courtnee said, "Any time you are, Pennington."

"I'll be back in five minutes," he told Ashley.

"I'll keep tidying up."

***

Courtnee's lightly spiced perfume was even more noticeable in the confined space of the elevator.

"Is that Jimmy Choo perfume you're wearing?"

"Why, yes, it is." Surprised, she said, "How did you know?"

"Good nose." He tapped the side of it with his index finger. "Kind of a hobby of mine."

An instrumental version of Warren Zevon's *Werewolves of London* played from small elevator speakers.

"He was brilliant," said Pennington.

"Who?"

"Warren Zevon. *Werewolves of London.*"

"I don't know him. I like Adele."

It's a good thing she's cute because her taste in music sure leaves a lot to be desired.

"If I recall correctly, he died back in 2003, when he was only in his mid-fifties. I think the reason I like that song is because I've always liked werewolf stories, even as a child. They were normal people until something was triggered in them to make them a monster."

That hung there, without further response, or even acknowledgement.

Exiting the elevator, even at such a late hour, people were milling about in the lobby, most talking on their smart phones or texting. Uniformed delivery men from two different pizza restaurants were waiting to be sent up to their customers' units. Pennington escorted Courtnee to the enclosed vestibule between the lobby and the porte cochere, where the valet's stand was located. A neighbor's new Rolls Royce was temporarily parked under the porte cochere. Although Pennington could afford one if he wished, being environmentally conscious, he wouldn't have dreamed of it.

"Just look at that thing. I understand they get about eleven miles to the gallon in city driving. Can you believe anyone would drive one of those gas-guzzling behemoths in this day and time? I mean, what are they thinking?"

"They're not," Courtnee responded. Although she wasn't as upset about it as he seemed to be.

Penningon surreptitiously palmed a ten dollar bill to the valet and thanked him for his trouble.

"Good night, Courtnee. Thank you for coming. It was a pleasure meeting you. May I have your number? So I can call you?"

"Thank you again for inviting me. And, yes, I'd love for you to call me. Just get it from Ashley. She'll know it's okay."

"Will do, then. Good night."

Even though he would have liked to have had more, he gave her a sisterly kiss on the cheek and returned to the elevator. After his ride to the top and keying the lock on the door to his home, "So?" Ashley said curiously.

"So, what?"

"What happened?"

"Nothing happened. I'm a gentleman. And besides, there wasn't a lot of opportunity with so many people milling about in the lobby."

"I guess, but she said I could give you her number, so you'll probably get your chance. I'll text it to you so it'll be in your phone."

"Again, I'm a gentleman."

"Pennington, please. You're a man. Given the chance, you will take every advantage."

He shrugged and gave up on what he knew was a losing battle.

Pennington sat on the sofa while Ashley tidied up the kitchen. "You know what I'm going to do next week?"

"What?" Her hair swinging in that direction when she turned to look at him.

"Well, even though I was born and raised here, there are many local sites I've never seen. I'm going to visit some of Atlanta's more famous local landmarks. Make up for lost time."

"I think that would be good for you, Pennington. I think you'd probably enjoy that. I only wish I could take a couple of days off. I'd go with you. But this is a huge time in real estate, everyone wanting to get into their new homes before the holidays."

"I wish you could too, Ash. But you have to do the work while you can."

"I'd say the party was a success, though. What do you think?"

"I feel like it was pretty good. I was pleased with the quality of people and the number that turned out. I mean, most of them probably haven't been to a party put on by a serial killer before. That probably made some of them come."

He didn't tell her about Warner's behavior. He remained a gentleman, after all.

"Pennington, stop it. They're your friends and they know you were exonerated and they support you." She collected her purse and coat from the bedroom. And got her iPad. Pennington started to give her the Bluetooth speaker.

"No, remember, I bought it with your card. It's yours."

"Oh yeah. I forgot. Thanks I really needed it."

Chapter Seven
Tempted

Making the decision not to limit himself to greater Atlanta only, Pennington decided to drive north toward the mountains, the view of which he'd enjoyed from his terrace but had never visited, and check out a new winery some of his guests had been talking about Saturday night. Both his guests and Ashley had raved about Fainting Goat, the newest of the more than seventy wineries that called Georgia home. The mountain and hillsides in the north part of the state provided the cooler temps, proper soil and good drainage needed for a wide variety of grapes to thrive.

Tuesday morning Pennington hopped into his small Japanese hybrid and aimed it mostly north for the less than an hour and a quarter drive to Fainting Goat Winery on the asymmetrical outskirts of Jasper, GA. He had to use Apple Maps on his iPad as a guide since the windy back country roads in the mountains were completely foreign to him.

Remembering that the frightening movie *Deliverance*, based on the even more frightening novel of the same name by the great Atlanta-born writer, James Dickey, and set as it was in the same north Georgia mountains, unnerved Pennington slightly on the drive.

Pennington arrived at the less than two-year-old winery and the first of the Georgia wineries he'd ever visited, in short order. A beautiful setting on a mountainside with an east-southeast view, he was pleasantly surprised at the level of sophistication of the facility. Hand-distressed, wideplank wood floors and a stacked-stone fireplace that filled half a long wall, was welcoming in the cool early-fall temps. A massive, elegant mahogany bar was on an adjacent wall and added to the beautiful setting in which to enjoy a glass of good wine. A two-story wall of windows looked out over the hillside vineyard. In the wonderful cool early autumn weather, he decided to sit outside at a high bistro table on the winery's ample deck.

Two employees were decorating the fireplace and all shelves with pumpkins and orange, yellow and red faux leaves.

Only a handful of people were enjoying the delicious wine in the pleasant setting on a weekday. *I'll have to bring Courtnee here sometime when she isn't working.*

Pennington had only one flight of four one-ounce pours of

different wines. Less than one average size glass of wine. He couldn't over-imbibe since he had the long drive back to Atlanta through the winding mountain roads. He finished his flight and put it on his American Express Black Card; then decided to begin the drive home. A quarter mile from the winery, he stopped at an overlook on the side of the road which offered a south-facing view, through a part in the mountains that even though it was over fifty miles away as the crow flies, allowed him to see his own building.

Wow, that's cool.

On the meandering drive south, Pennington dialed Courtnee's number.

"Hi darling. It's Pennington. How're you doing? Are you too busy to talk?"

Courtnee took a sip from a Diet Coke before responding. He noticed the pause and thought it meant she didn't want to talk. "I'm having a great day. How are you?"

"That's good. I'm fine. Thanks for asking. I was just wondering if you might want to have a glass of wine Thursday night. I hope it's not too short of a notice. I know women sometimes want to get a manicure, or get their hair done, or something."

"No, I'm good. I got a manicure before your party. That sounds awesome.

"Can you text me your address? Is eight okay? I'll pick you up."

"It's perfect! See you then."

The old Pennington didn't often attract pretty girls, so he was excited about his date with the super-cute Courtnee.

***

Unaccustomed by his prison stay to sleeping late, he came to and looked at the time on his phone— six o'clock— then rolled over and forced himself to sleep in until eight-thirty. Figured it couldn't hurt him to look fresh and rested for his date. After cooking a veggie omelette for some protein and healthy fiber, about noon he went downstairs and got a workout in the condo gym, to give his muscles a little extra pump and raise his energy level. Then, back upstairs for a leisurely wash in his shower, with its underlighted, white, plexiglass floor. He turned up the handle controlling the water temperature until steam billowed and the needle-prick sting was almost too much to bear. He consoled himself with the knowledge that he wouldn't get shivved or forced to perform, or be the recipient of, what was for him, an unnatural sexual act. He got madder by the second as he washed his arms, wishing he could scrub away the sleeve tats Bad Penny had gotten that were a rude and constant reminder of everything Bad Penny had done and he'd been through because of it.

Out of the shower he applied a pre-shave skin conditioner. Then came his favorite shaving cream with skin conditioner and as soon as he finished the shave, and while his skin was still wet, he applied a post-shave skin conditioner. One of the best things about being out of prison was having his personal hygiene products. Clipping errant nose and ear hairs with his new rotary trimmer was a treat due to being unable to keep them under control while in prison. He felt human again.

Applied old Spice deodorant then moved over to his dresser and retrieved his newest favorite cologne, Tom Ford Tobacco Vanille, from his assortment of expensive fragrances. He'd only discovered it since his return and already women and men alike had asked him what it was and paid him compliments.

Pennington dressed in a new outfit—brown worsted wool slacks by Versace, a navy blue vee-neck merino wool sweater over a white button-down dress shirt, then a muted brown and rust Giorgio Armani wool flannel sport coat. He was happy for the cooler weather that had arrived so he could inconspicuously wear long sleeves covering the stupid tats Bad Penny had gotten. He had already stopped wearing the diamond studs and was letting his ear piercings grow together. He wore the Breitling wristwatch he'd found in his leather valet where he'd left it on his nightstand. Not nearly as expensive as the six figure Patek Phillipe Celestial, but it was a fine timepiece and he didn't want to overwhelm his date with an ostentatious display of wealth, since she was a working woman.

Employed as she was in the real estate business, Courtnee had an imaginatively decorated early twentieth century cottage which she'd bought with Ashley's assistance. Pennington pulled up at 7:58, allowing himself two minutes to get to the door and ring the bell precisely at eight o'clock.

"Pennington, come in, how are you?

"I'm just fine, thank you. You look fabulous, positively gorgeous."

She was dressed in a skirt and sweater, in the latest fall colors, from Century 21.

"Thank you, Pennington. Would you like a drink?"

"Thank you, but no. We should probably be on our way."

"Okay, by the way, where are we going?"

"Red Sky, a tapas bar with dueling pianos. Have you ever been there?"

"I've heard of it, but no, I haven't."

"It's been around for almost ten years. And it's pretty popular with people in the Sandy Springs area or anybody that likes live piano music. They tend to draw from all over. It's not far, but it is a wee bit outside the perimeter and the music starts at nine, so we should probably head that way."

"Whatever you think."

Approaching his new Prius, Courtnee said, "Nice car, Pennington."

"Thank you, darling, I only drive it because I want to be environmentally conscious."

"Well, you're doing a good job of it."

Once outside the perimeter, northwest of Perimeter Mall, Pennington turned west on broad, six-lane Johnson Ferry just as an ambulance passed negotiating the heavy traffic. One of suburban Atlanta's busiest thoroughfares, it was slowed even more by an automobile accident and the accompanying blue lights. Crossed the Chattahoochee River and a moment later pulled into Red Sky's strip center parking lot.

With the street lamps and neon lights from the businesses the parking lot was well lit. They were hurrying across the asphalt to avoid the heavy rain rapidly advancing from the west, when a used-up man in his fifties neared. He'd just left a small market. "Ya ain't got a light, do ya?"

"Sorry, buddy." Bad Penny would have had one, but not Pennington Wentworth, II. "Did I fall asleep and wake up in the 60s? You never see that anymore. I wonder if he carries a white handkerchief, too."

"I know. Right?"

"Speaking of a light, matches have kind of gone the way of the dodo bird, haven't they? We use clicker firestarters with fire logs to start our fireplaces. If people do smoke they use the cheap throwaway lighters. You know, I miss matches. I actually liked the smell of sulphur."

"Ashley told me you were weird. Just teasing. Don't get mad."

The wind kicked up like it will on the front of a thunderstorm. More like a late summer storm than early fall. The refreshing fragrance of the approaching rain streamed on the air, barely beating the drenching maw of the storm that was slamming the front of the building just as they reached the entrance, Pennington guided Courtnee with a gentle but manly firm hand in the small of her back, as he opened the door. The same woman from the last time he had been there greeted them. He thought her name was Tracey.

"Welcome to Red Sky. Table for two?"

"Thank you," said Pennington, "but we'll sit at the bar if you don't mind."

Red Sky smelled the same as it did the last time he'd been there over a year before. Carpet cleaner and wood polish mixed with the aroma of spicy tapas, beer and perfume. The smell of fresh rain wafted on the air as others entered behind them. "Walk this way," he said, gesturing toward where the bar to the right of the entry dominated the medium sized room. A bachelorette party was in full swing in their private room in the corner behind the bar. The live music had already begun on the small stage at the opposite end of the café, starting with a beatbox version of Sir Elton's Benny and the Jets. The red walls and ceramic red-shaded lights suspended above the bar, with the dark wood and matching trim made for a warm, comfortable setting.

"Wherever you like."

"Pennington, long time no see," Stephen, Red Sky's only male bartender said, as he dumped a huge clear plastic bucket of ice into a polished aluminum bin to be used in cocktails, then fist bumped him as soon as he set the now empty bucket down and they sat on the back side of the bar so they could face the musicians without turning around. A tall, good looking young man in his late twenties, over six-foot three, Stephen had three day's growth of beard, and long dark hair tied back in a man-bun.

"Good to see you, too, bro. Yeah, I've been away. But I'm back now." Pennington guessed he must not read the Atlanta Journal and Constitution or watch local news or he would have known where he'd been.

"Well, we're glad to have you back. Dude, you been working out?" Stephen worked part time as a physical trainer at a nearby gym.

"Thanks, brother. I'm happy to be here. Yeah, a little." So far, Pennington was still managing to maintain most of the muscle he'd put on during his time in prison. He was already looking forward to the warmer temps of summer when he could wear short sleeve polos and show off his biceps and triceps. Of course he'd have to find a parlor to remove the tattoos Bad Penny had gotten that painted both arms.

"Well, it's working for you."

The dueling pianists played everything from Journey to Van Morrison to country songs, Eminem, the latest hits by Bruno Mars, Pink and the latest hip hop tunes. The crowd grew more enthusiastic with each number. And as the crowd continued to grow the temperature grew warmer.

Next came Charlie Daniels' "The Devil Went down to Georgia." On a rainy night in Georgia it was the perfect song for the time and place. It was a crowd favorite and it seemed like every guy in the place knew all the words. Loudly singing along with it. Thunder and lightning acted as the rhythm section for the pianos. Always equal opportunity musicians, they followed it with "Rocky Top," the University of Tennessee's theme song. But "Georgia On My Mind" got everyone pumped.

"What do you want to drink?" asked Stephen.

Always quiet, Courtnee said softly, "I'll have a glass of Chardonnay."

"Dealer's choice?"

"Can I have a J Lohr?"

"You've got it. What about you, dude?"

"I'll have a Firebird," Pennington said.

"This place is wonderful, Pennington. Thank you for bringing me here."

"You're very welcome. Thank you for joining me."

Stephen brought over their drinks. "Cheers." Noticing his date's drink, Pennington had forgotten that their wine glasses didn't have stems. He assumed that they broke fewer glasses and saved money that way, but being a wine enthusiast, it meant he didn't like them. Blood coursing through one's hand would warm up a white wine in a stemless glass rendering it undrinkable to an enthusiast. And grease from food coating the glass would obscure the colors of the different varietals. As with a with a lot of particular wine drinkers, Pennington thought that seeing the hue of the wine was half the pleasure of enjoying it.

"Cheers, Stephen. Thank you, my friend."

"He seems nice," observed Courtnee.

With a grin, and thinking he's funny, Pennington said, "Yeah, he's not an asshole." And, "we used to hang out sometime. He wants to be a writer."

During a short break in the music a particularly large blast of thunder rattled the large plate glass windows.

"How you doin'?" the guy on the other side of Pennington asked. Dude looked like a blue collar worker, muscled, in good shape. Difference was, from his time in prison Pennington didn't look down on that type any longer, and with his new muscles and the confidence that came with them and with the confidence borne out of surviving his stay in prison it seemed that men didn't demean him as much as they did his former self.

The piano players started playing Billy Joel's *The Piano Man*.

"Just fine, how about you?"

"Same. I'm Mike."

"Pennington."

"Nice to meet you."

"You, too."

"Cool place."

"Yeah it is."

"What do you do?"

"Just got back to town after being away for awhile. Looking. You?" Pennington didn't want to tell people he had been in prison or that he was independently wealthy and didn't need to work to live.

"Freelance long haul driver. Eighteen wheelers. I'll deliver a load to a certain state, pick up another load while I'm there and take it somewhere else. Always try to have a full trailer so I'm making money anytime I'm driving, everywhere I go."

"Cool, moving packages, freight, what?"

"Well, last week I made a freight delivery to Jersey, then went to the Meadowlands, met the circus and picked up four lions in cages and delivered them to Vegas."

"No, shit? That's about the coolest thing I've ever heard."

"I shit you not. That was a first for me. And I have to admit. It *was* pretty cool."

Even though there wasn't a dance floor at Red Sky, that didn't stop four or five young women who hopped up, made their way to the front of the small stage and started dancing, anyway. One of the pianists told the crowd they were first-grade teachers, always the wildest in any crowd. It was one's birthday, and their young charges would have been incredulous and wide-eyed to see them gyrating together.

The women stopped dancing and headed back to their seats when the intro to the following song, *Angel from Montgomery* written by the poet-master John Prine and originally recorded by Bonnie Raitt, and not a good dance song, brought down the house.

"I don't mean to play twenty questions on a first date, Courtnee, but are you from Georgia—Atlanta?"

"It's okay, Pennington. No, Hattiesburg, Mississippi. Even graduated from the local school, the University of Southern Mississippi. BS Degree in marketing. How about you?"

"I bet you were a cheerleader. You're cute enough to have been one. But, I'm Atlanta born and raised, UGA grad, Literature."

"I was one in high school. So, Literature degree—do you write?"

"No, I had dreams of it when I was in school, but life has a way of throwing you curves. I have visited Oxford, the land of Tolkien and Lewis, though."

A guy sitting three stools down the bar gave Pennington the willies. *He looks like he's been in prison. A real badass, probably a serial killer.* The creep made Pennington worry about the girl he was forcing a conversation on. He could tell by her body language and the look on her face that she would have moved to another seat had there been one available. The scene made him think of the line from the cool song by Twenty one Pilots, *Heathens*, from the movie soundtrack of Suicide Squad —*"You'll never know the psychopath sitting next to you. You'll never know the murderer sitting next to you."* He wasn't dressed appropriately for a nice place, in dungarees, a dingy white tee, a denim jacket over it. The top edge of a faded, green-ink tattoo indicating how old it was, barely visible above the neckline of the threadbare tee. The main tell to Pennington however, was his yellow-stained, gapped teeth that indicated many years of treatment, or lack thereof, by poor quality prison dentists. Probably only in his mid to late forties, he wore a silver Fu Manchu mustache he'd probably been cultivating for twenty years, the only thing changing about it the color of age, and his shoulder-length, straight, prematurely silver hair tied back in a ponytail, gave him the visage of an older man; the hard, lean cast of somebody who'd spent a lot of hours pumping iron and had a look in his eyes of a predator who wanted to harm someone, or worse, inflict pain for no other reason than because he would revel in it. Probably using power tools since he looked like a mechanic. Or throw somebody off the I-285 bridge into the Chattahoochee River late at night, leave him floating face down. A deep vast hole inside, he couldn't kill enough to make himself whole.

And from the lingering sneer the rough man gave Pennington it appeared that he'd sensed something of the same in Pennington—probably around the eyes. Ex-cons say they never lose the look in their eyes. The look of both predator and prey.

Pennington, lost in thought, began to recall things he didn't want to think about and gradually, falling into a trance-like state, lost all time and situational awareness. An almost total blackout.

"Pennington…Pennington… Are you in there? Are you okay?"

Momentarily somewhere else, he came out of it to Courtnee, with a concerned look on her face, gently jostling his arm.

He emerged from it glassy-eyed. "Yeah, I'm fine. Just zoned out there for a minute. How long was I that way?"

"Probably two minutes, and you had a…confused, look about you."

"It's nothing. Don't you fret." Pennington then downed the rest of the potent cinnamon-flavored liqueur and clunked it on the bar. And after dabbing his mouth properly with it, wadded up the black paper cocktail napkin and stuffed it in the small highball glass.

"Okay…if you say so."

"I say so. Now, let's enjoy ourselves. Stephen, two more." He held up his index and middle fingers also known as the universal sign of peace.

"I wasn't thinking," he said to Courtnee. "We should have Uber'd it. Then I could keep drinking. But since I'm driving, two is my limit." No more than an hour after arriving, Penninton said, "Speaking of that, since it's stopped raining, maybe we should think about leaving after we finish these drinks. Don't want to keep you out too late on a school night."

"That's very considerate, Pennington. Whatever you think. We'll have to remember to take Uber next time."

He missed the obvious signal that indicated her level of interest and a sign that she desired a second date. Truth be told, Pennington was a bit distracted by his black-out. He paid the lion deliveryman's tab without the guy being aware of it before they left because he thought that the working-class stiff was a cool dude and he still wasn't used to men not dissing him like they did before, due to his previous feminism. He just thought it was a gentlemanly gesture for him to do.

As they walked to the door, the piano players launched into *Don't Stop Believin'* by Journey.

"You know, I think Arnel Pineda is even better than Steve Perry was."

"Who's Arnel Pineda?'

"The Filipino singer who took Steve Perry's place as lead singer of Journey when Perry lost his voice."

"I didn't know about that."

"That's understandable, darling. A lot of people don't because Arnel sounds just like him. Most people can't tell the difference. He was singing in a Journey cover band in Manila, Philippines, when the remaining Journey members found him on YouTube and hired him to take the previous front man's place." Pennington was being considerate because he was beginning to think he might like this girl and he didn't want to risk making her feel dumb even though he felt sure most people knew about the change.

Courtnee twisted and curled a light caramel-colored strand of hair around her finger while lightly biting her lower lip.

Her signals of interest were too subtle for Pennington. He just had not had enough experience with girls to get it.

***

When Ashley entered the Buckhead office she couldn't wait to ask Courtnee about her date with Pennington. She entered the open door of Courtnee's office.

"So, how was the date," she asked, sing-songy.

"You haven't talked to Pennington to see what he said?"

"Oh, I knew what he would say. He'd say he was crazy about you."

"Well…I like him, but I don't know if I'll go out with him again." She gave her friend a chilly smile.

"Why not?"

"Ashley, he killed all those people. I don't know if I can risk it."

"Courtnee, that part of his brain is gone. If I were concerned I wouldn't have resumed my friendship with him and I certainly wouldn't have introduced you. You and I are friends. And the Supreme Court of Georgia woudn't have overturned his conviction or released him if they thought there were a chance he could relapse."

"Okay, *uncle*. I might give it another try. But I could just as easily go the other way."

"Well, I think you should give him a chance, but that's your decision to make." Ashley understood her co-worker's reticence but she was more convinced her old friend was back to normal.

Chapter Eight
Life

After partying too much and drinking too much alcohol in the form of wine most of the weekend at Buckhead dance clubs Friday and Saturday night and mimosas at Alon's brunch Saturday morning, Pennington decided to take it easy on Sunday.

With Bad Penny's vacating of him, Pennington recalled that he was indeed a practicing Catholic and decided to go to Mass. A small church he knew he hadn't been to before so hopefully no one would know him or recognize him. He liked that Catholics drank real wine and not grape juice at communion and only wished the Mass was still spoken in Latin. He loved the history and tradition of the church and thought something was lost when they changed it to English. He loved the celebration of mass.

It comforted Pennington to know that the music at Catholic Churches hadn't improved while he'd been away. The Protestants still sung way better. But he had to give the Catholics credit for one thing. They certainly had good donuts and coffee after mass. And after considering the attractive young women he noticed in the parish, he decided to mingle for awhile.

Returning home, Pennington changed out of his church clothes and deciding to chill on a beautiful autumn Sunday afternoon; he put on a white heavyweight cotton terry-cloth bathrobe with an embroidered logo on the left chest from a resort winery in Napa Valley. The General Manager had given it to him the last time he was there because he'd bought so much wine.

He started watching a Harry Potter marathon on SyFy, and with a new taste for protein from his time in prison, after being a total vegetarian before that, he decided to cook herb roasted chicken breasts for an early dinner.

While preheating the large Thermidor oven to 375 degrees, he retrieved garlic cloves, rosemary, thyme and organic Greek olive oil from the pantry. He summed up his personal theory of cooking with, 'If all else fails, add more garlic'.

Dehydrated as he was from his weekend of too much wine, he sipped from a plastic bottled water as he chopped the three cloves of garlic, rosemary and thyme on a wood chopping board carved into the image of the state of Georgia. And then, startled by the sensation that he was watching himself chop, Pennington set down the knife. It had been the state of Georgia that put him in prison, where Orpheus had taught him the Confucian principle that a knife could be used to kill or used to slice vegetables, *and don't get any ideas, Bad Penny.*

He then combined the ingredients in a small bowl, thinking that if the recipe had included parsley and sage it would make a great pop song, then arranged four chicken breasts he'd purchased at his neighborhood Trader Joe's on a large cooking pan, and sprinkled them with the chopped herbs and salt and pepper. Slid the pan into the huge oven and set the digital timer for thirty minutes. The popular high end supermarket was across the road and a block down from the other high end market, Whole Foods. Most of the employees had known him since before his prison stay. He liked Joe's, as he called it, better, except for its wine department. Whole Foods' was way larger. As a consequence of his incarceration and eating protein for the first time since high school he decided he'd have two of the breasts for his dinnner and save the others for another meal or two later in the week.

While the chicken breasts roasted he retrieved two bunches of broccolini from the huge crisper drawer in the bottom of the honey colored, wood-front Viking refrigerator. In a large bowl, while he whisked together two tablespoons of white miso paste, two tablespoons of olive oil, one tablespoon of soy sauce, a tablespoon of grated fresh ginger, a clove of minced garlic, and tossed in a pinch of black pepper, and a quarter teaspoon of red pepper flakes, he hummed a tune from a Broadway musical, with songs by Josh Groban. He then added the broccolini to the bowl and tossed the mixture, and slid it into the oven with the chicken breasts for fifteen minutes.

With the breasts and broccolini cooking Pennington snatched a fresh apple from a large bowl of fruit on the counter. Biting into the crispy delicious red, it crunched loudly and sprayed juice on his hand and all over the black granite counter top.

At the same time Pennington continued to prepare and work on his dinner, Harry, Ron and Hermione were trying to avoid Professor Snapes's menacing glare, on the widescreen tv in the sunken living room, he could see from the open galley-style kitchen.

Afraid of bruising them with his new prison-created muscle, and being careful not to apply too much pressure, he rubbed them with the garlic mixture, and filled the shallow pan with an unoaked Chardonnay while drinking the same from a large glass. Pennington liked to joke that he loved cooking with wine and occasionally even put some in the food.

Three days later, although he'd tried to fight them off, he had recurring thoughts of the guy at Red Sky he thought looked like a serial killer.

After thirty minutes he removed them from the oven and slid them under the preheated broiler. He removed the chicken breasts three minutes later, when they were golden brown, proud of his culinary accomplishment.

The warm aroma of roasted chicken and exotic spices filled his home comfortably on a cool autumn Sunday afternoon and Pennington ambled to the terrace to enjoy the pleasant weather and arranged a place setting on a bamboo placemat on the glass, hightop bistro table from where he could see the Peachtree Rd. traffic twenty-four floors below, and the mountains to the north. Then, returned to the wine fridge inside and withdrew a bottle of Nickel and Nickel chardonnay and all but lovingly caressed the bottle before unscrewing the cork and pouring a full glass, then, carrying the bottle of wine, the glass and the plate on a tray, went back outside and on the placemat set the wine and the roasted chicken and miso broccolini. Back in his penthouse, being back in his world of fine wine and good food, instead of eating the terrible stuff they masqueraded as food in prison.

***

It had been over six months since Atlanta Police detectives Nick Ramsey and Anthony Townsend, aided by some fine police work by Savannah Police detective Jordan Lynch, had caught serial killer, Pennington Wentworth, II, and they weren't happy to hear of his successful conviction appeal and release from the Great State of Georgia's care, when everybody knew he'd committed the dozen murders.

Townsend entered the squad room, a couple of detectives, in early and known even more than most detectives, as men of few words, said, "Mornin," without looking up. As dark and hard as obsidian. Tall and lean, he wore a moderately-priced Italian suit in dark gray with chalk stripes with a purple knockoff designer tie. He preferred to invest his money on better quality shoes and a nice watch and his daughter's needs. Today the shoes were shiny black leather Bruno Maglis. The watch a Tag Heuer. The firm leather soles slapped lightly on the tile floor.

Hearing the sound of his footsteps, a youngish detective with long blonde hair, who looked like a surfer, mumbled, "Dude."

Energized and enthusiastic about starting the week, Townsend greeted all of them with a friendly, "Good morning."

He entered the bullpen of desks that looked like every other PD bullpen in the country except this one had fabric covered dividers used to dampen the sound and arranged in a maze of ten-foot square cubicles and said to his partner, "Good morning, *mi amigo*." Ramsey's cube was as messy as his clothes. The prototypical rumpled detective's uniform.

Even though a cleaning crew came in every weekend, the squad room still smelled of stale cigarette smoke, albeit cigarette smoke mixed with industrial strength cleaner. Everyone knew there was a state law banning it. However, nobody had yet figured out how to get policemen not to smoke in government buildings. They all felt like they were above the law. Especially Ramsey.

"What's good about it?" Ramsey had never liked Mondays much and in fact since his second wife left didn't like most days, in general. He really had loved her even if he had cheated on her. It had only happened the one time, with a coffee shop waitress from where all the men on the job hung out. She had been his only affair…shouldn't even call it that. Call it what it was, a momentary loss of his usual good judgement—a one night stand, fueled by working long hours, dealing with the brass, the thugs, being unable to talk about the shit on the job, a want for some strange after feeling like he'd been married his whole life. But he hadn't been her first cop. Probably most, if not all the other detectives in the precinct had hit it. But he'd gotten caught and Lois had left. Wouldn't even discuss it with him. Just stomped out, and slammed the door, and he really regretted it. What made it worse for him was that considering his TV detective Colombo-like looks and rumpled clothes he knew the chances of him finding anyone else, certainly of Lois' quality, were slim.

He'd even seen the department shrink about it and everyone knew cops hate to talk to shrinks, even if the shrink is a brother—or sister—cop. And other cops would worry that if he were really fucked up they couldn't count on him when the shit hit the fan. Fortunately he knew he didn't have to worry about that with Tony.

"It's too early in the morning for you to be acting like that. You just had the weekend off. How can you be in a bad mood?"

"Believe me. It's easy. The weekend wasn't long enough. It was my Saturday to have Blair. She cried when I took her home. I'm tired of being a part time dad, the ex busting my balls, the assholes we deal with, dealing with the brass, the bullshit. I've got a better question. Why *aren't* you in a bad mood? Oh yeah, I forgot. You're the golden boy."

Truth was it bothered Townsend that his partner was in a bad place. He knew how much Nick loved his daughter. As much as he loved Samyra. Blair was nine and since Nick became a dad later in life, it may have bothered him even more.

He didn't want to upset his partner so he said, with his tongue firmly in his cheek and a grin on his face. "Just living the dream, partner." Even though African-American, tall and lean like a GQ model, and although without the long blonde surfer dude hair, Townsend was known as the golden boy around the precinct because he was squeaky clean and because of his felony close rate.

He added, "Hey partner. Why don't we give Jordan a call. We haven't talked to her since Wentworth's trial.'

"That's a good idea. She's a nice lady and a damn fine detective." The Savannah, Ga. female detective was the major reason they'd been able to get the murderer. She'd gotten a picture of him walking on the sidewalk on the riverwalk, thought he didn't smell right, and using good instinct sent them the photo, and pulled together a team of Savannah detectives and unis who helped track down Pennington and make the collar.

"Yes she is," said Townsend as he tapped her name on his cellphone, put it on hands free, and set it in the middle of Ramsey's desk. The desk had cigarette burns around the top's edges from generations of detectives in the nation's oldest continuously operating police building, using it as an ashtray. It reminded Anthony of his father's, minus the cigarette burns, in the corner of the den in their small house, when he was a kid. His father had loved that desk. "He'd said, "A man ain't really a man if he ain't got a desk." Anthony had remembered that and kept a desk in the corner of the living room in the small apartment he and Samyra shared.

She answered before the first ring ended. "Jordan Lynch."

"Jordan, Anthony Townsend and Nick Ramsey, here."

"Guys, long time, no hear. How are you?"

"Great, Jordan," Nick said, "How's our favorite chick detective?"

She changed her tone, just to make him think she was pissed off. "You never change, do you, Ramsey?"

"You wouldn't love me anymore if I did."

"Anymore?" She said with exaggerated incredulity, "That implies I loved you at some point."

"Ouch," said Townsend. He loved it when someone else busted his partner's balls. He didn't like having to do all the heavy lifting by himself.

"How's Cyndi Lauper?" Townsend was a follower of motivational speaker, Tony Robbins and always remembered family members—of friends, other officers, informants, even perps, after meeting the family at trial. He always remembered family members' names and asked about them. And he remembered the beautiful gray Maine Coon feline with a face and mane like a lion, that Jordan loved and thought of as family.

"Ah, you know. She's a cat. She wants everything on her terms. How's Samrya?"

"Twelve going on twenty-one."

"Aren't they all? Nick you haven't said much. How are you?"

He pulled a pair of cheap reading glasses from his inside jacket pocket and slid them onto the end of his nose before answering. He had to have them to talk on the phone. He figured there was probably some deep-seated psychological reason for that. If he ever had to see the department shrink again he'd have to remember to ask her about it. "Same old same old."

"Good, I'm glad to know some things never change."

"Hmmph. We just wondered if you heard that our guy, Wentworth was released."

"I heard rumor of it but I thought it was just the guys giving me the business, so unless you guys are in on the joke it must be true."

"Oh, it's true,"Townsend chimed in. "Obviously his attorney

convinced the Supremes that some other personality, or ethereal something-or-other committed the murders so they didn't stick a needle in his sorry ass, and kicked him out."

"Shit."

"Our sentiments exactly."

"Well, I hope he doesn't show up down here, again or I'll have to kick his worthless ass and throw it in jail again."

Nick said, "Only if there's anything left after we get through with him."

"Well, leave me something, then. I need to take out my frustrations with men on somebody." Same as with a lot of cops and probably even worse for women, relationships were a challenge at best and impossible at worst. With a resemblance to Angelina Jolie, and thirty-five, she got plenty of interest from men, but nothing that she encouraged. She wouldn't get involved with another cop. That would be a shitstorm of biblical proportions she didn't need.

"Will do, Jordan. Come see us."

"Next time I come to Atlanta to get a manicure and go clothes shopping I'll let you know. We can have lunch."

"Sounds good," Townsend said, "Do you like Mexican?" Even though he didn't look it, Townsend was a big eater. Most cops are. Meat and potatoes, it was part of their image.

"Doesn't everybody?'

"That's how I feel. And I know the best Mexican in the ATL. And their frozen Margaritas are strong as shit. But I'll warn you in advance. They will give you a serious case of brain freeze. They usually make my eyeballs hurt."

"That's the way I like them. I'll be in touch." Then she clicked off without saying good-bye.

"Damn, partner. Why'd you have to tell her we'd take her for Margaritas? You know I don't drink that Mexican piss." An Irishman to his soul, all Ramsey drank was beer or Jameson.

Townsend shrugged. "You don't have to go."

***

Orpheus seemed mildly depressed both to himself and everyone around him. Truth be told, he had enjoyed his time spent teaching The

Bad Penny, and now, a month after his release he was missing his young charge. He'd felt more alive than he had in years. He missed the energy. He summoned his bodyguard-confidante, Gage.

"So, your sentence is up at the end of the month." It wasn't a question. Thursday was the last day of Gage's sentence.

"Yes, Orpheus. You know it. We've both been looking to it with trepidation."

"I'm afraid, my friend, that I need to call on you further. I hope, although you aren't obligated, that you will indulge me. And obviously you'll be compensated for your loyalty."

"What do you wish of me, master?"

"I want you to look after our young friend, The Bad Penny, Pennington. I'm concerned about him. I'd like you to keep an eye on him, make sure he doesn't get into trouble. He paid me handsomely for my protection while under my care and I will take care of you out of that."

"Whatever you wish, Orpheus. What are your concerns?"

"I knew I could count on you. Your loyalty will be rewarded in this life or the next. I'm just afraid for his safety if he gets involved with an unsavory element, and if he does, I'd like you to...ahh...*discourage* them from causing our young friend any harm. Oh, and feel free to acquire any assistance if you so need. But at the same time, try not to do anything that will cause you to end up back in this shithole."

"Count on it, Orpheus. Consider it taken care of. I won't need any help. And I'll do my best." Gage had never been one to lack confidence, especially when it came to kicking ass. It was just something he'd always been good at, going back to the first time he'd had to put an ass whuppin on another kid in second grade for licking his finger and touching Gage's chocolate cake with it at lunch. Too bad no universities offered a course of study in being a bad motherfucker or he would have stayed in school, graduated magna cum laude and gone on to graduate studies in the field.

"Fine, but remember, if you need any help, get what you need and I'll fund it."

Gage rolled his eyes at Orpheus' repeating his offer. Like, "Please."

***

A pair of days later, continuing his tour of greater Atlanta sites, Pennington decided to visit Stone Mountain Park, the state of Georgia's most visited tourist site, on the north side of the huge granite pluton bearing the largest bas relief sculpture in the world, early on a Tuesday morning. Approaching the park, the confederate generals Stonewall Jackson, Robert E. Lee, and Jefferson Davis on horseback, on the north side of the large granite rock—loomed large over the quaint southern village of Stone Mountain.

Desiring a leisurely visit, he opted for the gondola ride to the top rather than attempting the strenuous mile long hike up the mountainside. He purchased the ticket that would allow him to gather with others to wait for the tram to depart.

After giving the cashier his Visa, since they didn't take American Express, which made him slightly miffed, Pennington made his way toward the Skyride. He meandered through the Civil War-look southern village of souvenir shops, theatres, picture booths, restaurants, past three restrooms and even passed a coffee shop advertising Starbucks on an aluminum exterior wall sign that had been hand-distressed to give it an authentic 1800's era look. School children on a field trip with the teachers accompanying their charges yelling at them to slow down and hold hands, ran past him, almost running him over. A young boy of ten or eleven trying to draw out the last vestiges of an Indian summer, with the last ice cream, but losing the battle in early November and a nip in the air, ambled by with the sugar cone double dip running down his sleeve to his elbow.

Before reaching the queue for the ride, one was forcibly routed through a large souvenir shop riminiscent of its kin at DisneyWorld. Hawking tee shirts and caps of various colors, postcards, coffee mugs, and various gifts, trinkets and mementos, all bearing the image of the Confederate generals for which the park was famous. They determined to drain you of all possible cash and encouraged you to go to the snack counter to buy a soda—coca cola products of course—it was Atlanta, after all.

By chance he took the longest walk of the several circuitous routes to the Skyride boarding point, and by the time he got there, impending bad weather caused park management to make the decision to shut down the ride to the top. Literally giving him a raincheck, and seeing as how he'd never been to the top, Pennington would have to repeat the process the next day.

***

After making his way past the same shops, cafes, theatres and hucksters, and crossing the great lawn where visitors sat on lawn chairs and blankets to watch the nightly laser show on the side of the mountain, before finally reaching the Skyride, Pennington had to wait online with a queue of people, some local, some, obviously, due to the different languages overheard, international visitors, eager to see one of the south's most famous attractions, for a few minutes, to catch the gondola. He wound through the path of polished stainless steel bollards. Workers cut off the line three people behind him, making the others wait for the next run of the tram with a capacity of no more than thirty-five. Only a short ten minute ride to the top, but the view of the height would have been nerve wracking for him had it not been for the calming sight of a beautiful pair of Red-Tailed Hawks soaring on the drafts, that served to relax him.

Arriving at the top, and exiting onto the concrete platform at which the gondola docked, the first thing to gain Pennington's attention was the aromatic fragrance from the evergreen trees, pines and cedars—mingling among the hardwoods changing now to their autumn wardrobe of colors to form a partial covering on the otherwise bald granite surface. That and the sharp chill wind on which the fresh scent carried. He turned up his jacket collar, listening to the happy chirping of birds.

The wind was way stronger on the mountain than on the ground over eight hundred twenty feet below. "Damn, this footing is worse than I figured." The round top looked like the surface of another planet, except where the autumn-colored deciduous trees and pines looked like a Rocky Mountain forest. With his legs and balance still somewhat impaired from the car accident, the uneven surface was a bigger challenge than he'd expected. *Good thing I didn't try to make the climb to the top. That would have been a mistake. Wish I had a hiking stick just for walking around up here.*

As he walked through the souvenir shop the lone security guard he saw on the mountaintop was distracted by the cute young woman he was chatting up. In the store, he bought Ashley a bracelet with the images of the generals on it. He knew she'd never wear it—the trinket was too cheesy—but it was proof that he'd been thinking of her and because she was raised well, she would have the good manners to pretend to appreciate it.

And after putting the small bag in his jeans pocket, he went to the mens' room to take a leak, then bought a bag of popcorn in the snack shop. Wandering aimlessly, he munched on his treat and enjoyed the inspiring westward view of the Atlanta skyline—the four discrete areas of downtown, midtown, Buckhead—where he could make out his own condominium building— and perimeter. He then walked toward the flimsy chainlink fence that was a weak barrier a third of the way down the steep slope, intended to keep people from getting too close to the even steeper slope on the other side, dropping off to the edge of the cliff that was a shear fall above the carving in the wall of the mountain below.

As he neared the rickety barrier a young Asian woman caught his eye. She appeared to be attempting to position herself for the perfect selfie.

"Tess?"

"Excuse me?"

"I'm sorry. My mistake. You remind me of someone." The young Asian woman Bad Penny had murdered and left on fire in a dumpster in an alley behind the Marriot Marquise in downtown Atlanta.

"I don't think we've met. My name is Mei Ling. I'm in my first semester at Georgia Tech, IT major. Since the weather is so beautiful— I love the first cool temperatures of fall. They remind me of Beijing—I just decided to take a break from my studies this morning to do a little sightseeing."

"How nice. I'm Pennington, Penny. So you're by yourself?"

"Yes, none of my friends even know I came here.They wouldn't be happy with me if they knew. They think I'm too trusting."

Perfect. thought Bad Penny. He'd already seen the sole security guard distracted by a cute girl. They were alone. Losing consciousness and situational awareness again, this time due to the surprise of seeing someone he thought he'd murdered, wasting no time, he moved quickly and silently until, within striking distance and quickly balling his muscular hard right hand into a fist, punched her in her delicate mouth, breaking her flawless white teeth and knocking her out. The last sensation her brain registered before she lost consciousness was the salty metallic taste of the blood in her mouth. He caught her collapsing body before anyone could notice, and lifting her above his head, threw her unconscious form over the fence where it rolled on the softly sloping surface to the brink, until it tumbled over the edge of the cliff, then, twisting in free fall and curving toward the face of the mountain, where it impacted with the massive granite back of Robert E. Lee's horse, Traveler, and she left all of her face and half her brain, in a smear of red and gray on the stone, until the body went into freefall again, finally landing on the ground over six hundred feet below the horse's back.

Still confused, Pennington's face morphed into a mask of rage. *Fuck! Fuck! Fuck! Why did she have to make me kill her again? She should have just stayed dead.*

Glancing around surreptitiously and trying to be cool about it and hoping to counter any undue attention, he made sure no one had been paying him any mind. It was apparent no one had or he would have already heard sirens arriving at the scene below and people on the mountain scrambling, as if they could do anything. Too late for that. Pennington wandered around the mountaintop for a few minutes with the intention of calming down. Taking that time, his brain returned to normal and with it he forgot what he'd done, and so had no sense of urgency to get away from the crime scene.

I guess I should start home. If I leave now I can stop somewhere for a nice lunch and a glass of wine on the way.

But Bad Penny had returned!

With his mental state returning to Pennington, life was back to normal and he forgot about the mayhem that had been committed. He took the next gondola to the bottom and back-tracked the way he came down the path passing the shops, restaurants and theatres. Back on Interstate-285 going north and west toward Buckhead.

***

Deciding to stop at one of his favorite fern bars for a bite, he ordered an arugula salad and a quiche Lorraine and had two glasses of Pinot Grigio.

At home, another glass of wine and the fresh fall air on his terrace reminded Pennington that life was good. He decided to watch one of his favorite movies, Pride and Prejudice, because he liked the Mr. Darcy character since he knew that all women like the image of the ultra-strong alpha male. The four hour movie had ended by the time the eleven o'clock news came on.

In the old days, before prison, if he wasn't out partying, Pennington would try to catch the local news at eleven. He thought the weeknight news anchor was cute and he figured that hundreds of newscasters in smaller markets would kill for her job in one of the nation's largest cities, and he guessed she was hoping for a move just across town to CNN's headquarters, to a national job. He thought he should attempt to put himself in a place to meet her, maybe at an important local fundraiser for charity, or at the High Museum or some other such function. He knew that most people fortunately were so fixated on their own lives they didn't notice the things or people that didn't affect them directly, and he was already finding that to be true in his own situation.

The "teaser" before the commercial introduction indicated there had been a tragic accident at Stone Mountain, but Pennington wasn't paying attention. He'd been in his wine room uncorking a bottle of Reisling and didn't hear it.

After pouring himself a glass of the syrupy unctuous German wine he returned to the living room. Pennington's favorite anchor, with a dire look on her immaculately made-up face, told everyone in the television audience that a Georgia Tech student, a young woman from China, had apparently gotten past the barrier fence intended to keep anyone from getting too close—they guessed she was trying to get the best selfie possible in front of the sixty mile view —to the edge and slipped and fallen off the precipice, impacting with the carving on the wall of the mountain before landing in a copse of pine trees at the foot of the state of Georgia's most popular tourist site. Her name was being withheld pending notification of her family in a suburb of Beijing.

As the story unfolded Pennington started to get a sick feeling in the depths of his bowels. And even though at the moment he was Pennington—not Bad Penny—he seemed to recall, although it was more like a conscious nightmare than a recollection, that he had been at Stone Mountain that morning and what he had done during his second blackout in less than a week.

He changed the channel, as sometimes he would watch *Jimmy Kimmel Live* after the news, but getting a punch in the gut from what he remembered he decided to go straight to bed. Although shaky with realization and dread he was able to flounder weakly to the shower before brushing his teeth and stumbling to bed.

The ambient light from the moon and from other nearby buildings kept his bedroom from being absolutely dark. The frames of the bedroom windows cast dark shadows on the ceiling. They looked like the ones from prison cell bars cast by moonlight. They weren't as bad as in prison, however. It was never full dark in prison, for security, and the shadows were everywhere. He fought to keep out the images of the day's evil he'd done. He clamped his eyes shut against the shadows of his mind. With the vision of prison, his thoughts turned to Orpheus and the feeling that he never wanted to disappoint the great man. But it was troubled sleep.

"Pennington, why'd you kill me again? You're not Bad Penny anymore. You're supposed to be better than him. Why'd you do it? Why?" He didn't know if it was only a nightmare, or if it were Tess, or was it Mei Ling, speaking to him.

Kicking the covers off, "Son of a bitch," he screamed, waking in sheets pooled with cold sweat and his skin covered in chill bumps.

He finally forced himself into disturbed slumber.

The next morning, tiring of his own coffee and desiring a better nutritional start to the day than he could make, and after dressing in a pair of trendy skinny jeans and a v-neck orange cashmere sweater over a rust and brown-plaid Polo dress shirt, he decided to visit Alon's again, the European-style pastry shop, coffee bar, European market and wine bar, that was an old favorite, for a latte' and a fresh fruit Danish. His second time in in less than a week, employees remembered and greeted him.

"G'morning," he responded to each of them politely. The wood fire blazing in Alon's pizza oven looked as warm and inviting as a family fireplace.

Sinatra was singing a song Pennington didn't recognize on their sound system.

Several large bright orange pumpkins and gourds of green or white decorated the floor and displays of food, wine and other goods for the autumn season.

The warm air of Alon's was a universe of heavenly baked smells. Looking over their vast array of fresh baked goods, Pennington decided on a raspberry-cheese Danish and a large skim milk latte' with two stevias. In the old days he would usually have something healthy like real steel cut oatmeal with genuine butter and fresh berries but now, out of prison, he intended to live a little and indulge his sweet tooth with both food and drink.

He found a table. It was decorated for the season with a cheerful centerpiece of five small orange and green gourds. He took a bite of the sweet Danish and washed it down with a large mouthful of the equally sweet latte' from the ceramic mug he'd requested instead of their usual paper cup. The delicious pastry was sticky and messy.

Well, that decides it., If Bad Penny is going to return, it will be up to me to keep us out of prison. He's not clever enough to do it himself, and it seems like he's only going to make momentary occasional appearances, anyway, so, it's left to me. He has good instincts and common sense, but I've always been the smarter one, no matter what he thinks. And gazing at the classy European-style surroundings and enjoying his food and drink, although accustomed to eating faster from his prison stay, and fortified with carbs and caffeine, he continued to think.

And I musn't...
I just can't leave this life again.
I can't go through that hell again.

***

He walked toward the restroom at the rear of the market/restaurant to wash the sticky remains of the delicious pastry from his hands and then, making the decision not to deprive himself, returned to the display case and bought the blueberry scone that had made his choice of a pastry difficult a few minutes before, to go. It was given to him in a small white sack, and without a care in the world, he all but floated out the door and to his car. Life was excellent...except that Bad Penny was back.

Pennington seemed to be settling into a routine.

In prison, bored to tears, he'd learned to entertain himself with only his thoughts. Now free, with books, movies, and a car he could get into and just explore, he knew he would never be bored again, and wondered how anyone could say they were.

Still trying to restock on necessities and fashion in new sizes due to his physical change during his time in prison, he decided he'd go to Lenox Square, probably the most exclusive mall in the southeast, and Atlanta, known as the land of malls. Louis Vuitton, Mont Blanc, Burberry, Diane Von Furstenburg and Prada called Lenox their home in Atlanta.

But, first he'd call Courtnee.

***

Detectives Ramsey and Townsend arrived at the breakroom at the same time.

"You had any caffeine yet?" Ramsey asked his partner.

"Only the crap I make at home."

"Well, this won't be any better, but at least I'm buying."

"Sounds good, hook me up. By the way, did you hear about the news at Stone Mountain yesterday?"

"No," Ramsey said, pouring his partner a cup."What happened?"

"It was all over the local news: a Georgia Tech student, a 19 year old young woman from China, apparently went over the edge, tumbled down the face. Killed on impact, if not before that, from bouncing off the wall. Only speculating, but they think she was trying to take a selfie."

"Get the fuck outta here. When will they learn, God love 'em."

"I know. It's terrible." Townsend shook powdered sugar, creamer and two Sweet 'N Low packets into a styrofoam cup. "Her poor family."

"Yeah, I can only imagine how her parents feel. Two days ago life was good. Their daughter was in an excellent school in the U.S., trying to make a better life for herself so she could send money home to her family. The next day; their lives will never be the same."

"And just think if it turned out to be something else. It could have the makings of an international incident."

"Don't even think that way." Ramsey took his coffee black. Thought that was the way a real cop should drink it. He eyed Townsend's cup's mud-colored contents with over-exxagerated-

disdain.

"It sounds like somethin' our man, Wentworth, would do."

"Yeah, but he's rehabilited now, back to a normal productive citizen."

"I'll *rehabilitate* his ass." Detectives were used to tuning up suspects when they knew they were guilty. Thought nothing of it. Regardless of coffee preferences. Everybody did it and no one ever saw anything.

Ramsey said, "Only if you let me have an assist."

"You got it, partner."

***

Pennington rang his friend, Ashley.

"Hey Ash, what's up?"

"Just working. What's up with you?"

"Well, I just called Courtnee and got the cold shoulder. I asked her out again and she turned me down. She had enough class to give me a reason, but I can read people well enough to know it was an excuse."

"Oh, Pennington. I'm sorry. I talked you up. Tried to convince her she should go out with you again."

"Hey, it's okay. I get it. I'm a serial killer."

"Pennington, stop."

"I think I might check out some of the dating websites." Using the television remote to scroll through movies while they talked to see if there were any he might want to watch.

"Might not be a bad idea. Everybody's doing it."

"That's what I understand. Guess I'll give it a go."

Clicking off with Ashley, Pennington turned on his iPad and Googled "online dating."

***

After looking over a few sites he decided to join "Take Your Pick." Before he could do anything else on the site he had to set up his own profile. Deciding it was going to take awhile he retired to the terrace, cool autumn air and colors of the season painting the countryside.

Settling into one of the chaises on the terrace, he pulled up the site again and answered the most basic questions—age, height, hair color, body type, drink or no, what one likes to do, hobbies, what he was looking for in a potential mate, etc—and uploaded five pictures. So far so good, but now it got tricky.

He decided to use a nickname, just in case any of the women were to recognize his real one. He was pretty confident they either hadn't seen or wouldn't recognize him from his picture, and he hoped once he met someone, if they did, his name wouldn't matter. He was clever enough to figure something out when the time came, if it did. Finished, he uploaded his profile, and pictures, and decided to hit the town.

He dressed in what was becoming his go to autumn uniform—skinny jeans, brown and rust plaid long sleeve shirt with a brown tweed wool sport coat covering it and Timberland short laceup boots. A classy outdoorsy look. He decided on Opera Atlanta on Peachtree Road again. Being humpday and all, he figured that on a Wednesday there should be a pretty good crowd. He was glad to see there were quite a few attractive women at the bar, most head down staring at their smartphones, probably updating Facebook, and sipping the latest designer cocktails. Martinis of various flavors, New Old-Fashioneds, and Manhattans; tres chic and very sophisticated. An open seat between two pretty young women made his decision easy for him, as he slid the barstool back and eased into it, as cool as could be. With a preference for brunettes over blondes, he turned to the girl on his left. It was a no-brainer for him.

"Hi, I'm Francis, Francis Hentworth." He'd long thought that if he ever had a son, he'd buck family tradition and give him the name Francis. And he'd name a daughter similarly spelling the same name with an "e".

He enjoyed his newfound appeal with the opposite sex. It gave him the aplomb to approach them, which made them like him even more.

The odds were anybody he met in a bar wouldn't be long term, but if it turned into something he would tell them later that he was using an alias just because girls like to gossip about guys.

"I'm Taylor. Nice to meet you." Exotic and sophisticated, she could have been of Spanish, or Italian heritage. A man would have to earn her trust before she'd open up. One could tell she was a very closed woman. Her dark sensitive eyes however, were soulful and expressive, telling one more than she would want you to know.

"It's my pleasure. So, your parents were James Taylor fans?"

"You guessed it. But, at least they didn't name me 'Fire' or 'Rain.'"

"That was really funny. You have a great sense of humor."

"Thanks, but that wasn't the first time I've used it."

Her glass was almost empty. "What are you drinking? You need another one? "

"You don't have to do that."

"I'm happy to. What are you drinking?"

'That's so sweet. A French martini."

"Sounds good," and to the bartender, "Barkeep, another French martini for the lady, and I'd like a glass of your best Chardonnay." Before he became "Bad Penny" he wouldn't have dreamed of calling a mixologist barkeep, but Bad Penny wasn't bound by polite convention and it seems that some of that was now ingrained in Pennington, and, it seemed, that at least some girls liked it.

"You got it."

A moment later, her cocktail arrived and after one taste, *Despacito* by Justin Bieber began on the club's sound system. He took a sip of the chard and said, "Cakebread…not bad."

"Would you care to dance, Taylor?"

"I love this song. I'd love to."

"Yeah, it's pretty cool. Let's do it."

Another good dance tune, Bruno Mars' 24K Magic, was next up so they stayed on the floor. Pennington's moves were no worse for the wear from his time in prison. He could see the chicks checking him out.

Returning to their seats, they slowly sipped their drinks and made small talk while getting to know each other. It had worked pretty well when he told someone he had just returned to town, and was looking for a new position, so he thought he'd try it again.

"What kind of job are you looking for?" Taylor said.

"Well, I majored in Literature at UGA, so I'm not really qualified for anything, but I'm self taught in IT, so that's the area in which I'll focus." That was a new twist to his story. He decided to use his own educational background instead of making up everything from scratch, just to try and make it easier to keep straight if she asked any questions. Sounded like something Bad Penny would come up with.

Taylor revealed she was in finance with a large local bank.

Pennington had heard horror stories about first dates or the first time meeting girls where they pulled out their phones showing photos of their kids, dogs, or unable to talk about anything but their mother and fortunately Taylor did none of that. Even though he thought she was hot, he would have had to invent an excuse and get the hell out of there if she had. But at least he would have been gentleman enough to have invented a good excuse.

"Speaking of work, I better think about leaving," Taylor said. "Six-thirty comes pretty early."

They exchanged phone numbers and weighing being courtly with not wanting to come across as too forward he decided not to offer to walk Courtnee to her car.

"Could you possibly see me to my car. It's getting late and I'd rather not go out in the dark alone. There could be bad people out there."

How ironic. "I'd be happy to, milady."

Fortunately for her, Bad Penny didn't seem to be be reappearing.

She had parked her newish black BMW 3 Series in a lot across the street. Pennington said, "Nice car."

"Thanks.I just bought it. Used. It's a '15. My daddy taught me to always buy a late model used car."

"Your daddy's a smart man."

"Where are you parked?"

"In the next block. Not far."

"Hop in. I'll drive you."

"You don't have to."

"I insist."

"Allrighty, then," He always liked that line when Jim Carrey said it, "But only if you insist."

"It's settled, then."

He helped her into the driver's side then jogged around to the passenger side. She popped the remote lock to let him in.

The sweet purr of German technology when the engine engaged in response to the ignition made Pennington a wee bit jealous. The illumination from the dash bathed her features in an ethereal sickly green glow.

"It's the silver Prius on the right,"

"That's a nice car."

"Thank you, but it's no Beemer."

She pulled up behind the Japanese car, slid the gear shift into park and looked at him with sensitive, intelligent eyes. She was almost encouraging him to make his move. "Thank you for making it such a nice evening."

"You're most welcome." And he leaned over, cupped her cheek in his right hand and kissed her passionately. It was different from Bad Penny's first appearance. This time Pennington was aware of Bad Penny's arrivals and because he disappeared after satisfying his blood lust, Pennington hoped that the killer wouldn't return.

When he pulled away first, she said, "Wow. How'd you learn to do that? You kiss like an Asian. Her hand came to rest between her breasts in disbelief.

"Just lucky, I guess."

"Well, good night, Francis. Call me?"

"What do you think? Good night." As he stepped out of the car, since he made up his name on the fly, using reverse psychology, he said, "But you should probably Google me before we go out, just to make sure I'm who I say I am."

"Oh, Francis, it's nice of you to offer, but I don't need to do that."

His idea worked. On the drive home, he basked in the afterglow of that kiss. *She likes me!* He looked forward to making it to second base.

Turning on the entry light before going in further, he then went straight to the shower. He looked longingly at the claw-foot tub since before he went to prison he was a bath guy. But after prison and all the changes he'd experienced he considered a shower more manly, and he flipped the switch turning on the lights underneath the white plexiglass shower floor. It gave the entire bathroom a soft glow. Glass block walls enclosed all but the step-through opening. Since it seemed he could look forward to more attention from the opposite sex, he was hopeful of sharing the shower with someone, soon. Even though he'd never had any luck with girls before his change he'd had the romantically large shower built with that in mind.

Enjoying the hot water, and the clean fragrance of his men's shower gel, he then brushed his teeth and all surfaces of his mouth before flossing.

As somebody who had always been hot natured and unconcerned as he was about bugs on the twenty-fourth floor he opened the door to the terrace letting the cool, crisp autumn air in to freshen up his condo. Although Ashley's housekeeper had been there only a few days before and it had a clean smell, he liked the fragrance of fall that the outdoors brought with it. Climbed in between the clean bed sheets sans bedclothes. He loved the feel and smell of the perfectly washed and dried sheets from his favorite scented laundry detergent and fresh smelling fabric softener. The blankets and scratchy sheets in prison certainly didn't smell like this. He thought about Taylor. He wished she were with him. He always went to sleep on his right side gazing out his bedroom window at the dark silhouette of the mountains sparkling with the warm yellow lights from homes against the lighter night sky sprinkled with the sugary white sparks of stars.

Sleep came and the dreams started. "Pennington, Pennington, it's time to pay the piper. You don't think we got you out of prison out of the kindness of our hearts, do you?" "We need a stone-cold killer." An evil cackle followed. "You owe us. And believe me, we shall collect."

Pennington came to about three a.m. Not fully awake but not asleep either. Conscious enough to ponder, while shadows danced on the ceiling. Unable to decide if someone had been speaking to him telepathically or if it was just his imagination running wild with memories of the voice that had spoken to him at his conviction vacation.

Chapter Nine
Fertile Grounds/Killing Fields

The first full day of Pennington's online dating profile: He checked email at 10 o'clock and had notification of three "flirts" and a "want to meet."

He responded to all and although none of the interested women seemed to be his type in the "looks" department, it seemed that he had a few things in common with one, so he figured you never know.

***

"You've been a loyal friend, Gage. I'm happy you're getting out of this vermin infested pigsty but I shall miss your comradarie, your wit and your intelligence. Alas, I shall die in this God forgotten shithole. But, watch over our young friend until we're sure he's going to be okay and contact Mr. Wasserman when you need funds. I have asked him to set aside a substantial amount to keep you flush for the foreseeable future. Likewise if you should need my consul, talk to the attorney and he will facilitate it.

"Thank you, Orpheus. I won't forget you."

"After all this time I think you can call me Jon."

"Allright then...Jon."

***

"Tony, do you know anybody on the Stone Mountain PD? I'd like to know if they have anything new on the girl who went off the mountain."

"Yeah partner, couple of years ago, you were on vaca and a father kidnapped his seven year old daughter while on a visitation, and he ended up over there. I worked with one of their detectives on it. Good guy, Evan Tirk. Have his number right here," he said as he scrolled through his smart phone. "I'll give him a ring."

"Cool. Let me know."

He walked toward the restroom as he left a voice mail. "Evan, Anthony Townsend, APD, here. Long time. Hey, just wondering what's going on with the Mountain death investigation. No hurry. Call me when you can. Thanks."

"Left him a voice mail, partner. I know him. He'll get back to me."

"Thanks, brother."

***

Following the unwritten but thoroughly adhered to protocol of not calling a girl the next day for fear of appearing too interested or worse, needy, Pennington didn't call Taylor the following day but waited an additional twenty-four hours. So, since it was Friday, even though he was running the risk that she already had plans, he asked her out for Saturday night.

"I'd love to have dinner tomorrow night, Francis. Thank you."

"Wonderful. I can pick you up or we can meet, whichever makes you more comfortable."

"I'd be happy for you to collect me."

"Sounds good. Can you text me your addy?"

"Of course."

"Pick you up at 6:30, so we can have dinner at 7?"

"Perfect."

"Okay. I'll see you then."

***

Since he'd enjoyed it so much with Ashley, he thought Taylor might like Il Giallo."

Dressed in a houndstooth gray wool sport coat over a v-necked sweater of olive green with an argyle pattern of multi-colors over his skinny jeans, he arrived at her door promptly at 6:30 with a single red rose.

"Francis, how sweet. You shouldn't have. But I'm glad you did.

'Nonsense. A beautiful lady should have a flower."

The greeter, who was also the general manager and co-owner, remembered him from his previous visit.

"Good evening, my friend. It's good to see you again." Leo, short for Leonardo, an Italiano wearing a dark suit over a heavily starched white shirt with a bright red tie, had a photographic memory and impeccable manners.

Fortunately for him the man hadn't learned his name the first night or it would have caused Pennington problems with Taylor.

Once they were seated Pennington ordered a calamari appetizer for them to share. Taylor then ordered a veal parmigiana for her entrée and Pennington the branzino, a whole, head on fish. He asked for a bottle of French white burgundy which would pair beautifully with both of their entrees.

A moment later the server arrived carrying the wine in a silver ice bucket on a three-legged stand. He offered Pennington/Francis a taste and he set the cork on the white table cloth and being a gentleman he deferred to Taylor.

"That's wonderful, Francis."

"I'm glad you approve."

The server poured each of them a glass, then after returning the bottle with the towel wrapped around the neck to the silver bucket, a different server arrived a moment later with the calamari appetizer. Each of them tried a plump calimari.

"These are the tenderest calimari I've ever had," said Pennington/Francis.

"Yes they are. They're delicious."

"Do you have any big plans for tomorrow?" He took another sip of the burgundy.

"It's supposed to be a beautiful fall Sunday."

"No firm plans but I was thinking about a hike in the mountains. It should be even cooler up there than here and perfect for hiking."

If one could lurk while sitting, a figure sat lurking at the bar. Pennington/Francis' back was to him, but had he been facing the man it's possible the figure wouldn't have been recognized by him with the dark beard tinged with gray, sunglasses at night and not dressed in prison stripes. He wore the shades at night not to look cool, but because he knew he was unable to control the intense look of his eyes and it was off-putting to some. His burning gaze took in everything, missed nothing. *Damn, Wentworth's date is hot. Not Asian but definitely an exotic look. Too bad I'm here to keep an eye on him, and not scout out new targets.*

Leisurely finishing their dinners, when the server came presenting dessert options, Pennington/Francis was disappointed that Taylor declined as it would have then been impolite for him to have the Tortino Di Ciocolatte he'd already spotted on the menu and wanted to try, unless he could talk her into sharing.

"Would you share a dessert with me? Something chocolate?"

I'd love to, but I really shouldn't."

"Well, only if you're sure."

Upon exiting the restaurant, the temperature had fallen and being gallant, he shed his sport coat and gently wrapped it around her shoulders without asking if she would like it.

"Thank you, Francis. How sweet."

Giving them a minute to get outside, and using some of the money he got from the attorney, Gage paid cash for his tab, two small glasses of sake which he ordered chilled, the way natives drink it in Japan, and a bottle of Kirin, a Japanese beer he was surprised to find the restaurant served.

Pennington drove Taylor to her home in Dunwoody. She didn't invite him in, but she did invite him to go hiking with her in the mountains the next day.

"That would be cool," he said. "What time should I pick you up?"

"How about eleven? By the time we get up there it will be early afternoon and not quite as chilly." Due to the elevation and being pretty far north, the mountains were always cooler than Atlanta.

"Sounds good. We can pick up coffee at a drive thru on the way."

Gage knew Pennington would have to drive his date home, so he returned to the mid price hotel less than a block, a two minute walk, from Pennington's condo where he'd taken a room. The room smelled of cigarette smoke and Lysol since housekeeping had at least attempted to rid the room of the smell. He'd been in prison so long he didn't even know he could have gotten a smoke-free room. It didn't bother him that much, though. And the mattress felt new and was firm. An inexpensive print of the Talmadge Memorial Bridge in Savannah hung over the bed's headboard. An overhead picture of Atlanta's Hartsfield-Jackson International Airport hung on the opposite wall. Watching with a small handheld monoscope he'd picked up at a nearby Goodwill store, he saw Pennington pull into his numbered parking spot just after midnight. *He must not have gotten lucky.* The hotel room was well-sited to keep a weather eye on Pennington's car in Pennington's parking spot to know whenever he's leaving and tail him. The only downside was he had to be up, dressed and ready to go on less than a moment's notice. And he was up, in the dark unfamiliar room, trying to avoid kicking a chair, or a dresser, or a desk leg and breaking a toe, then showered, dressed and had coffee by seven o'clock. *I'm sure that's early enough on a Sunday.*

Peering through the part in the blackout curtains, at ten-thirty five he saw Wentworth walking across the condominium parking lot to his Prius, a spring in his step and twirling his key ring on his right index finger. *Maybe he did get lucky.* The parking lot was shiny black asphalt and looked like it had been recently repaved, not patched. Their homeowner' association must have plenty of money. Wentworth wore a dark tan, fleece-lined, Carhartt suede vest over a matching long sleeve, tan canvas shirt layered with a dark olive tee providing an extra layer of warmth, tucked into Wrangler jeans cinched with a wide brown leather belt and lace up hiking boots. Brown leather gloves since it would probably be several degrees colder in the mountains.The only thing he lacked, didn't think about, because he never wore one, was a cap to keep his head warm. Other than that he looked like a real outdoorsman. Gage knew him well enough to know he was playing a part, an actor's role.

Gage walked out into the gray autumn weather. The sky was the color of the sea in Manila Bay where he'd spotted his first victim as she walked by the shore. It was still lighter than the darkness behind the blackout curtains in the hotel room. He looked up to where the halo of sun was trying to pierce the overcast. It made him sneeze.

As Pennington passed by, Gage looked the other way just to be on the safe side. Climbed into the small Toyota SUV he'd rented using cash at a no-name lot. Pennington couldn't possibly know his car, so he pulled in behind him and followed a block behind as he drove into the nearby Dunwoody section of Atlanta.

Pennington pulled to the curb in front of a one-story white colonial with green shudders flanking the windows. Gage pulled over a block away, from where he could watch the front door. A moment after Pennington's finger touched the chime the door opened and the girl from the previous night appeared. She greeted him with a kiss.

*** *

"Good morning, Francis."

"Good morning, darling. You ready to do this."

"Absolutely. You?"

"Morning couldn't arrive soon enough for me."

He took her hand as they walked down the sidewalk to his car, then he pulled away from the curb and went back the way he came and Gage ducked below the dashboard as they drove by. After they passed, he then made a two-point one-eighty degree reverse and followed them out of the pleasant middle class neighborhood. Quiet on a Sunday morning.

"So, where did you want to hike," Pennington asked.

"I was thinking a section of theAppalachian Trail near Blood Mountain."

"Perfect," and he turned out of Dunwoody and pointed his car north on nearly deserted hwy 400. The traffic on a Sunday morning wasn't nearly as bad as it would be on a school day.

At exit 6A Pennington got off on Holcomb Bridge Road going east. On the right at the first stoplight, there was a McDonald's on the backside of a Texaco service station and convenience store. Pulling into the drive thru he said, "How do you like your coffee? Could you eat anything?"

"Cream and one stevia. And I could eat a breakfast burrito."

He spoke into the microphone, "I'll have two large coffees, both with cream and one with one stevia, the other with two, a breakfast burrito, mild sauce; and a sausage-egg-and-cheese Mcmuffin."

Pulled up to the drive-thru window and the aromas of hot coffee, sausage and bacon cooking drifted into the car. The look on Pennington's face grew serious as he handed Taylor her food."Please forgive me if I was wrong. I assumed you would want mild sauce with your burrito."

"You assumed correctly. I don't need hot sauce," She had a naughty grin on her face as she said it.

Getting the subtle joke, Pennington agreed, "You sure don't." In seconds they were back on Hwy 400 with the hybrid Prius pointed north toward the mountains. Although he'd never let on, he was secretly excited since he'd never been hiking or to the mountains except to visit Fainting Goat Winery a week or so before. He told

Taylor to rest her cup in a console cup holder. With his iPhone sitting in the dashboard cupholder where it was plugged in to charge, he place his cup on the seat between his legs.

As he drove he keyed Blood Mountain—so named for a bloody battle between Cherokee and Creek tribes—into Apple Maps on his iPad and set the automobile's cruise control on what was for him, a conservative seventy mph on the broad six lane highway. Then, having moved some of Ashley's music to his iPad, he plugged it into the MP3 player and they were listening to a variety of music, new and old.

A song from Manchester Orchestra came on and he said, "Do you know them, Manchester Orchestra? They're from Atlanta."

"Yes, I've been listening to them for years. They're great."

After a few minutes of listening to music they both realized they didn't feel it necessary to talk. Comfortable just being with each other.

About forty miles north they passed on the right, the ancient furniture store with the large sculptures of the pink panther and his female companion lounging on the grounds in front.

"Aren't they ridiculous?" asked Pennington/Francis."

"They are hilarious."

 Not long after that landmark, Highway 400 became Long Branch Road and narrowed to two lanes and not far after passing a trail-horse rental business, that road ended. In the shadow of a mountain, a dozen brown mares, a black horse, and a gray-dappled horse grazed in a small fenced-in corral next to a log barn with a United States flag draped over the door. Three of the mares were saddled, waiting for riders, while a small long-tailed tan dog played in the shade under a picnic table.

"I've never ridden before, but I think I'd like to give it a try," said Pennington.

"I did when I was a little girl at summer camp, but that was over twenty years ago."

That told Pennington/Francis that she'd had a privledged upbringing, maybe not as advantaged as his own, but nevertheless, substantial.

The further north they drove the land out the windows got hillier, then turned to low mountains, then they grew taller, almost before their eyes. Taylor said "I just love the mountains,".

"Me, too," he said, although he'd only seen them from his condo terrace.

The fall colors grew more vivid the further north and higher in elevation they traveled. A left turn, a right turn, past Frogtown Cellars and Kaya Vineyards, two popular north Georgia wineries, and another left, onto a winding mountain road leading them to the trailhead parking lot for the world famous Appalachian Trail that meandered from Georgia to Maine. A deliciously clear mountain creek mirrored the road the last few miles, even crossing under it once. Just past where the creek switched sides, was a campground half full with travel trailers and RVs. A beautiful setting on the creek bank. Although it was a sizable crowd of campers, it would have been full in summer.

They first checked out the hikers' outfitters store, Mountain Crossings, at Neel Gap, on Blood Mountain, sonamed for a bloody battle between the Cherokee and Cree tribes, A beautiful green trimmed stacked stone building originally built as an inn and over one hundred years old, it was the only structure on the entire length of the Applachalachian Trail through which the famous path passed. The owner allowed trail hikers to spend the night for a nominal fee in a separate part of the building still in the inn configuration with rooms, bathrooms, and showers. In addition to hiking boots, backpacks, sleeping bags, caps and other hiking and camping necessities they had maps, paperback books with stories about the area, clay pottery logo coffee mugs and a rainbow of tee shirts and sweatshirts that said "Paddle Faster. I Hear Banjo Music." A nod to the movie Deliverance, filmed not that far away in a further east part of north Georgia, based on the novel of the same name by Georgia's own James Dickey.

Opening the car doors the aromatic fragrance of Georgia pines floating on the the chilly autumn air, flooded the car.

Autumn didn't so much as creep up on Blood Mountain as much as arrive in an explosion of brilliant color that looked like it would last forever. But come December the beautifully painted tree branches would be naked, before giving way a season later to virgin green, until summer's arrival with the deep green of maturity.

Following the stone path to the entrance, they passed under a large tree in which hung from the limbs were dozens of hiking boots tied together by their laces in pairs, where hikers had thrown them after completing the length of the trail.

As they entered, a young Asian man and a young Caucasian woman—each no more than twenty—exited, packs on their backs, glistening with sweat and smelling like they could use a shower. They had obviously been on the Trail for awhile.

Opening the door to the store it smelled of old wood, damp stone, brewing cofffee and a huge fire in an enormous stone fireplace, original to the inn when it was constructed. At the first shirt rack she came to Taylor said, "I just have to have a "Paddle Faster" Tee, and a coffee mug with the AT logo."

"You need to get them, then."

"What do you think of the pink Tee?"

"It will be beautiful with your hair."

Pennington/Francis bought them each a hand carved rustic hiking stick. "It can't hurt," he said. And not knowing how long or how far they would hike he picked up a couple of nutrition bars and bottles of water.

"Why, thank you, Francis. I've needed one for awhile."

After making their purchases they got in the car and drove the half a mile further north to the trailhead parking lot.

He turned left onto the one lane asphalt strip, about two hundred yards long, not much more than a two-track, that fed into the lot. It was empty except for only one other car, a purple eighties model Camaro with bondo on the left front fender, that looked like it might have been abandoned there. Empty on a Sunday, probably because most people were watching football with the NFL season in full swing.

Pennington/Francis parked on the other end of the lot from the old car. Before getting out, he cinched the laces of his boots and Taylor smoothed her hair.

"Are you ready to do this?"Pennington/Francis asked.

"I'm always ready. Oh, wait. I should text my mom and my best friend. Let them know where I am. I forgot to let them know earlier."

"No problem. You should do that."

She looked at her phone, "Oh crap."

"What?"

"I don't have a cell signal."

"Well, we are kind of remote. You can try again when we start down the mountain."

"Okay, I guess that will have to do."

At the start of the trail, pine needles covered the ground. It's possible they'd fallen there organically, but most likely were spread there by the hand of man. The start of the path made one think of the clever tee-shirts with the saying "I Hiked The Entire *Width* Of The Appalachian Trail—a distance of about six feet. Rough, but flat at the beginning, it transitioned quickly to a gentle slope, fully enclosed by trees. The pleasing fragrance of the tall white Georgia pines was even stronger here on the path under the canopy of autumn colored hardwoods, the russets, burnt oranges and mustard yellows of red maples, sugar maples, different varieties of oaks, beech trees and ash. Someone who was outdoors all the time wouldn't even notice, but for Pennington or someone like him who doesn't go to the mountains often, the pine scent was pleasing and overwhelming. They made their way, deliberately. Within fifty yards, granite boulders began to appear, some no bigger than a football, others covered in moss and as large as a Volkswagen bus and every size in between.

The trail grew steeper, and the temperature dropped, as they ascended, the aromatic air growing colder. According to the weather report—given by another woman with a boob job—which Pennington had seen on TV before they left the city, it had been in the low fifties in Atlanta. But up here sixty miles north and at the higher elevation, he guessed it was in the mid to low forties.

"Aren't the colors magnificent?" Taylor had stopped, hands on her hips, gazing into the trees. The colors of the hardwoods were spectacular since until the present time autumn had been late arriving and mild. "Typically by this late in the season the leaves would have already turned brown and dropped. Even the trees in my neighborhood are amazing."

Pennington/Francis agreed. "They are pretty spectacular."

He decided to let Taylor set the pace, at the same time hoping she wouldn't move too fast causing him to have to ask her to slow down. About a mile later it seemed to be working fairly well. Pennington was in pretty good condition from all the workouts in prison and at least so far keeping it going in his condo gym. Even though the mountain was cold and a chill wind refreshing, Pennington/Francis was sweating profusely unlike Pennington had ever experienced, unaccustomed as he was to physical exertion of any sort except for his workouts.

He hadn't had to ask her to slow down and although he was getting a little winded it wasn't too uncomfortable.

"I hate to slow us down, but if you don't mind I'm going to go back behind that last big rock we saw and pee." Taylor was embarassed, but it would be even more embarrassing to wet herself.

"Of course not, darling. I'm sure I'll have to go shortly, also."

***

Taylor walked a short distance down the trail and disappeared behind a boulder the size of a kitchen, one end halfway buried beneath the soil.

She unzipped her designer denims.

As she squatted the sound of a twig snapping from a footstep to the left of her a few feet away.

"Well, well, well. What do we have here? With unnatural speed he was upon her clamping his meaty left hand over her mouth, but not before she screamed for help. "Francis."

Pennington/Francis sprinted toward the sound.

The interloper had already unbuckled his jeans and had begun the degrading assault.

"Gage, stop! What the hell are you doing here anyway?"

Without stopping the act, Gage grunted, "Orpheus wanted me to watch over you, Pennington. Take care of you."

"And this is how you take care of me?"

"I have to take care of myself sometimes."

Between muffled screams, Taylor said, "Who's Pennington?"

Covering his face with his hands, it painfully contorting into a cruel mask of rage, Bad Penny was making a return appearance. "No, goddamn you," Pennington yelled.

Pennington didn't know if he was admonishing Gage or Bad Penny, but Bad Penny won out, either way. The psychological transformation complete, he hoisted a granite stone, the size of two footballs, but with a weight of over one hundred pounds and in an imitation of an Olympian's clean and jerk lift, raised it over his head and with a roar of insanity, crushed it onto Taylor's head. Her protests ended with the explosion of teeth, hot blood and brain tissue, splattering artistically on Gage's clothing like paint on a dropcloth.

"Damn, Wentworth, what'd you have to go and do that for?"

His face clenched in a mask of quiet rage and confusion, and appearing as if he were Dr. Jekyll's Mr. Hyde, Bad Penny said,

"Pennington didn't do it. I did," he continued, "besides, you made me come back. This is on you."

"Yeah, well we can debate that later. In the meantime, let's get the fuck out of here."

His features easing and his tone softening, Pennington was returning from wherever he went when Bad Penny made an appearance. "Wait. We need to bury her. Or at least hide the body, if not take time for a proper burial—"

"Shut up! We don't have time. Besides, the animals on this mountain will take care of it soon enough." Indeed, Coyotes, bobcats, cougars and bears were abundant in this part of north Georgia. Pennington acquiesced.

Driving back down Blood Mountain and pointed south toward Atlanta, Pennington recovered his senses and remembered what Bad Penny and Gage had done. He pounded the steering wheel with his palm. "Crap! Crap! Crap!" Pennington still still didn't use swear words like Bad Penny, even though he was really pissed that he failed to keep Bad Penny at bay.

The wild animals didn't get to the nearly headless body before other hikers found it, but ugly black crows had begun to pick at the remains.

* * *

Before Pennington could make it down Blood Mountain, four sheriff's department cars, two each from Lumpkin and Union counties, since Blood Mountain was on the county border, raced up the mountain, along with a Lumpkin County EMT truck, all with emergency lights flashing and sirens screaming. They sliced into the parking lot, tires screeching,

The two Lumpkin County officers might have been twins, or at least their stomachs were. Both of them stretching the fabric of their brown uniform shirts to the breaking point. In their forties, they had the look of men who'd grown bored with the job and looked forward to anything that might give them some excitement. Even the tragic discovery of an almost beheaded young woman's body.

The older of the two started yelling at the pair of hikers who found the body and had had the good sense to call 911.

"Move! Get outta the way. You'll contaminate the crime scene." He spoke around a toothpick and wore mirrored tear-drop shaped sunglasses.

"Please," said the other deputy, "do what he says. It will save us all a lot of grief."

Even the EMTs weren't immune to his yelling.

"Keep that truck back. There's no rush. Nothing can be done for her now. You mess up my crime scene and I'll have your asses."

The male hiker said, "Okay, dude, no problem. It's just my girlfriend, I'm afraid she's going to throw up. She's never seen a headless body before."

"Can you help her move, then? That would for damn sure contaminate the scene. And you would really see him go crazy."

"Okay, dude. No problem," he said for the second time.

***

About that time, Pennington pulled into the North Georgia Premium Outlets Mall to throw up.

He opened the car door, leaned out and puked his guts onto the asphalt parking lot. *Crap. That tasted like shit.*

Pennington got home and turned in early after his long day of hiking and mayhem, even though Bad Penny had taken over and occupied his brain, it was still Pennington's body affected by the physical stress.

Once asleep, Bad Penny came to him in another nightmare.

"I have an idea how we can do this."

Pennington tossed and turned, sweating, *Do what? I don't want to do anything with you.*

"Too late, dude. I'm back. You and me, we're one. We're even closer than brothers. We're the same person."

Stop it! No, get out of my head!

***

"Morning partner," said Nick.

"Morning, bro."

"Bro?"

"Come on, man, lighten up."

Townsend's mobile rang. "Townsend here."

"Tony, Evan Tirk here."

"Evan, my friend, how you doing?'

"Excellent, except for girls falling off of mountains."

"Yeah, I hear you. Speaking of that, that's why I called. Anything new? Still an accident?"

"No, bro, nothing new, no reason to believe it's anything but a tragic accident, but how would you know? So, my gut, fifty-fifty. Why you askin'?"

"Oh, dude, you know, just a feeling in *our* gut. I don't know if you remember our serial last year, Wentworth, Pennington Wentworth? His conviction was overturned and he's out and my partner, Nick Ramsey, you haven't met him, but he's paranoid and a suspicious son of a bitch and he just wanted me to check with you, see if there was anything you guys weren't telling the locals."

"Yeah, I remember seeing that on the news. But what can I tell you? Maybe so, maybe not.

"I hear you, brother. Thanks a lot. If you need us don't hesitate to call."

"Thanks. Will do."

He turned to his partner."He says they don't know squat—50-50. Might be what it seems—an accident—could be a homicide. How could you know without witnesses when someone falls off a mountain.

***

Pennington got up and even though he was awake, Bad Penny's voice continued to speak to him

This can't be good. I'm awake and I hear him and I'm conscious of it.

"Good morning. Fire up your iPad. I have an idea."

I don't want to hear your ideas.

"Sorry, dude. Like I said, we're one now. Back, middle of last year you didn't know me when I first showed up. You weren't even aware of my presence until after I decided to leave. If you remember, I left the night before they were going to kill us. I couldn't have that. Or rather, they couldn't."

"Anyway, back to my idea. You signed up for that dating website. That was a great idea, by the way. A stroke of genius. That should provide us with plenty of opportunities. But, how about this? Get on one of the gay dating websites. You know, people always thought you were gay, anyway. Play that up and we can do some of them too. I still don't like those sons of bitches."

Pennington started brewing a pot of coffee.

In his brain, the voice of Bad Penny kept up a running commentary. *"You know, I like my coffee black."*

Forgetting momentarily that Bad Penny could read his thoughts. *Like I care what you like, you son of a bitch.*

"Oh, getting a little feisty, are we? I know I can't hurt you without hurting myself, but remember, I can hurt someone close to you, so you better mind your manners."

"Anyways, get your iPad fired up. We've got to get our profile on a dating site for fags."

Okay, okay, hold your horses. Then to himself: *How does one keep his thoughts to himself? When someone is a part of his mind?*

"How the hell do I know? You're the one who studied philosophy with that sensei dude. But you better goddamn well figure it out, 'cause if you piss me off you aren't going to like what happens. And you remember how you never knew I was there last year? You just disappeared when I took over? Well I think we're both going to stick around this time. Share the fun."

Another two minutes and the coffee was ready. Pennington put extra cream and stevia in his mug just to let Bad Penny know he was still in control.

"So that's the way it's going to be, huh?"

Fact was from his time as Bad Penny, Pennington liked black coffee just fine, but he had something to prove to his evil counterpart.

"Actually, it isn't that bad, but it would be better with some brown liquor in it."

It's eight o'clock in the morning.

"I know what time it is, dude. I'm just saying."

Pennington retrieved his iPad from his nightstand where he charged it overnight. He had to admit the idea of getting even with some gay guys who always thought he was gay, had a modicum of appeal to him, even though he thought murder was unquestionably over the line.

"Our main picture must scream 'effeminate'. Shouldn't be difficult for you. Sorry. Sorry. I'm just saying. Maybe one of you drinking a cosmo, or a glass of white wine or when you were ice skating Christmas before last. That sweater you were wearing was too cute for a man and should attract some attention"

I don't need your help.

"I have to admit you're right. You've got looking gay down, pretty damn good."

Chapter Ten
Upping His Game

With Bad Penny's less-than-altruistic motives and assistance, Pennington created his profile on the gay website, uploaded photos and waited for the response. Trying to do his best to keep from being caught as a murderer, he added "New in town, looking for another newbie to see the sights with." He hoped he'd meet men without many local friends, men that wouldn't tell others about their new friend and whose friends wouldn't promptly notice someone missing. He didn't have to wait long. It seemed that he was quite popular.

He arranged the date for two days hence.

Thursday night arrived and he dressed in one of his metrosexual outfits, a gray striped, cashmere, v-necked sweater vest, over a starched long-sleeved white dress shirt, and dark gray merino wool dress slacks and black tasseled, Bruno Magli loafers. And he spiked his hair with gel. They were to meet, as arranged, at The Eagle, one of The ATL's longest-running gay nightspots.

Pennington arrived fifteen minutes before the seven o'clock hour they'd agreed on so he could watch for his date to arrive and have a glass of wine to relax his nerves. The bar was dark, trying to create an intimate setting. It was the first time he'd ever tried to appear and act gay.

"What'll you have?" Asked a bartender, wearing black slacks, a white long sleeve dress shirt with bicep garters and a red bow tie.

"A house chardonnay," he said with a lilt. *I'm not trying to impress anyone.*

"You better try and impress your date."

So, you're still here.

"Damn right I'm still here. I told you doing this together could be a helluva lot of fun and we're going to make sure you know what's going on this time around. There sure are a bunch of fuckin' flamers in here, aren't there."

If anyone had been paying attention to Pennington when Bad Penny was "speaking" to him, it appeared that his face contorted in evil anger. When Pennington "responded," the same face was grievously distressed. Jekyll or Hyde. But no one noticed.

A couple of minutes after seven an atractive young man

approached Pennington at the bar. He was stylishly dressed in a slim fit black sport coat over a black tee shirt, black slacks and sneakers. At this point it appeared that gay mens' pictures were a more honest representation of their looks than straight womens' on dating websites.

The young man said, "Are you Francis?" Pennington had decided to use the same alias so he wouldn't have to remember too many names.

"I am. Bryan?"

"Yes, please to meet you. You look just like your photos." He leaned in for a gentle hug and, Pennington could smell his expensive cologne and cinnamon flavored mouthwash. He was soft-spoken and had the voice of a choir boy. And the looks of one, too, much younger looking than his early thirties. Like he was still in college.

"You, too. That's nice for a change."

"Thanks. Agreed."

"Can I buy you a drink?"

'I'd love a Blanton's manhattan.'

"Bartender, can we please have a Blanton's manhattan and can I have another house chard?

"Coming up."

"So, tell me about Bryan." If Pennington could get him talking about himself, maybe he wouldn't have to make up to much. Bad Penny agreed. *"Good one. Don't want to talk too much."*

"Moved here from Asheville, NC. Moved there for the arts community and loved it in the mountains. The cool weather was fantastic. I was originally from Columbia, SC. Undergrad and grad school at USC, the "real" USC. Too hot and not much in Columbia except Fort Jackson Army Base. Couldn't wait to get away from there. Wasn't for me. So, left for Asheville."

"I love Asheville," said Pennington.

"Yes, it's a really cool town, but I just decided I wanted a bigger city. And you? Where are you from?"

This was the part he hated. "Northern Virginia, DC suburb. But I can't stand politics. Had to get away after undergrad at James Madison.

Pennington spun his wine glass on the bar marking condensation circles as he talked but decided it was too masculine a gesture and, he stopped.

"I can understand that. Atlanta's big and cool."

"I think you're right. Hey, I need to go to the restroom. Be right back."

"Don't get lost."

"Hey, this is a target rich environment. Why don't you cut this guy loose and move on to more fertile pastures?"

Well, I was just thinking about getting a headache, but not because you say so. He's a nice guy. He doesn't deserve this.

Pennington studied the can lights hanging above the bar in the hope he might find the kindest words in them."Bryan, I'm sorry, but I think I'm coming down with something. I think I should probably go home."

"Oh, I'm sorry. Is there anything I can do? Are you sure?"

"I'm sorry. I'm sure. It'll be best for you if I just leave." *Little does he know.* But Bad Penny took over. "Hey we can do it again, if you like."

"Well, I was just thinking." He placed his hand on Pennington's thigh as he began. "Do you have plans for next week? Thanksgiving? I'm a great cook. I have a Martha Stewart roast turkey recipe. Don't you just love Martha? Of course I alter it. And I get the fresh herbs out of the container garden on my deck. I brought 'em with me from Asheville. I stuff the turkey with thyme, sage and parsley and lemon and orange halves, and baste it in butter and Chardonnay. How can anything cooked in butter and Chardonnay be bad? And my sides aren't too shabby either, dressing with sausage and pecans—an old New England recipe—sweet potato casserole and others. It's to die for, I promise. We can even roast chestnuts in the fireplace."

"That sounds real nice, Bryan." Bad Penny was was doing the talking, but as Francis. Looked like his plan could come together after all. "I'll bring the wine. I think Pinot noir or rose' are good with turkey and dressing. Why don't I bring both?"

"Sounds perfect. Alrighty, then. It's a date."

Even though it was difficult and against his nature, Pennington-Francis leaned forward and kissed the attractive young man on the cheek to say good night.

Bad Penny said, "I'm sorry I don't feel well. It was a real pleasure. I'll talk to you before next week." He waggled his cell phone at him.

"You better."

Several men checked out Pennington as he left. Bad Penny thought he would definitely have to come back.

***

On Friday morning, typical of late autumn in Atlanta, the skies were gray and the temperature chilly, in the forties. Pennington decided to do a little early Christmas shopping. Ashley was the only friend he needed to buy for, but he usually bought himself a nice sweater every Christmas and was thinking about buying her a nice cashmere sweater. Perhaps he'd buy himself one, too. His J. Peterman jeans and crew neck sweater were the perfect outfit for the weather.

Everyone knew Lenox Square was the best mall in the south, so that's where he'd start. Even on a Friday morning right after opening for the day when most people would be at work, the parking lot fronting Peachtree Road, described as Atlanta's Broadway, was full. Inside the front entrance was a massive artificial blue spruce Christmas tree reaching from the first floor to the ceiling of the second, covered in red and gold ornaments larger than softballs. Christmas songs filled the mall from hidden speakers. Arriving shortly after most of the stores opened at ten, on a chilly morning during the shopping season, he thought an eggnog latté at Starbucks would be a good way to start his day.

Starbucks was in the open area of the mall next to the base of the escalator on the first level where he sat able to see everything and everybody on the lower level. Santa Claus was a little further down the mall sitting on a golden throne with red cushions. On his lap, sat a little girl with yellow curls, crying, in a fairy tale-like, gingerbread-cookie North Pole setting. A young woman with the same yellow hair was standing nearby making sweet sounds and faces at her, urging the child not to cry so they could get a good picture. A line of moms with toddlers and babies waited for photos with the jolly old soul. Pennington could see that his long gray beard was real when the little girl pulled it. He heard a woman nearby, *sotto voce*, call him "Glenn."

Almost all of the tables were full, but he found one empty small table for two. He popped the case on his iPad and pulled up Google to see if anything newsie had broken about the murders. The death on Stone Mountain was still classified an accident and although people at the Mountain Crossings store remembered seeing the young woman, they couldn't place her with anybody. So nobody connected the two murders, or anyone—especially him—to them.

It wasn't long before Pennington closed his iPad and was instead watching a number of pretty and stylish women riding up and down the moving staircase.

"Talk about a target rich environment. I just thought that gay club was."

I'm ignoring you.

A pretty young woman, loaded with bags even though the mall hadn't been long open, stepped up to the counter and ordered a grande' skinny cinnamon dolce latte.' She scanned the area for a place to plop, but all the tables now occupied.

Bad Penny gestured to the extra chair at his table. "Would you like to sit down?" Bad Penny could be *almost* as charming as Pennington. With a tired sigh, she said, "Thank you, I'd love to. I was supposed to meet a girlfriend but she didn't show. And I thought she'd help me get all this stuff to my car So I need to prepare myself for that."

"Then I hope you'll allow me to be of assistance. I'm Francis, by the way." Bad Penny was in control.

"I'm Sharon. I certainly won't turn down such a sweet offer."

"Nice to meet you, Sharon. Just let me know when you're ready.'

"In about this long." She gestured with the red Starbuck's Christmas cup.

"So, what are you doing here on a Friday morning?"

"I just took the Friday off to get some Christmas shopping done, you know, beat the rush? What about you?"

Doctoral program at Georgia Tech, cut class this morning for the same reason."

"Really? What field?"

"History." It was the first thing that popped into Bad Penny's mind. Pennington was sitting there, sipping an eggnog latte as Bad Penny spun his web.

He took a sip of his eggnog latte' and she took the lid off her cinnamon dolce' and blew off the cloud of steam.

"Ooh, that's still hot."

"So what do you do for a living?"

"I'm a legal assistant in a large firm, over two hundred attorneys. They keep me pretty busy."

"I bet they do." Noticing she wasn't wearing a ring, Bad Penny said, "How about a glass of wine sometime?" He knew she wouldn't live long enough for that to happen, but he was trying to make her feel comfortable about her decision to walk out with him.

"That sounds lovely. We'll have to exchange numbers when we get to my car."

Pennington didn't like being aware of Bad Penny's actions. It was worse than the year before when Bad Penny took over and he had no knowledge of it. *I hate this helpless feeling whenever that son of a bitch takes over because I know there's nothing I can do about it.*

"You're right. There isn't."

"I think I'm ready to go, if you don't mind."

"Of course not. Where are you parked?"

"I parked out this side entrance over here." She gestured down the hallway to the right. "Far less crowded and more parking places."

"Sounds perfect," thought Bad Penny. He drew on fleece lined brown leather gloves to guard against the cold and the transfer of friction ridges, the scientific term for fingerprints he'd learned at his own trial, just in case the opportunity presented itself. He still couldn't be sure at this moment.

Pennington couldn't do anything but watch.

Picking up her assortment of designer bags from the finest stores Atlanta had to offer, he felt like a Grand Canyon packhorse, loaded down as he was.

Walking down the short hallway to the north entrance laden with bags, he worked up a sweat, since the heat was turned up in the mall to fight the outside chill.

"Excuse me?" she said.

"Oh nothing." He'd been singing along to the Chipmunks *Christmas Song*.

Almost no one else was parked on the second level of the parking deck, which boded well for Bad Penny's evil plans.

Approaching an impeccably cute, red, convertible Audi, she started to dig into her large Louis Vuitton handbag for her keys.

Distracted as she was, Bad Penny decided to use it to his advantage. Moving with puma-like quickness he pounced on her, grabbing her head in his vise-like strong right hand and slammed it into the juncture of the roof and the driver's side door. She collapsed unconscious. He grabbed her purse, found her car keys and, shoving her inert body in ahead of him, pushed her into the passenger seat and climbed in behind the steering wheel. He pulled around to the rear of the mall, and stopped near the Marta tracks.

Then, withdrawing the Swiss Army knife he'd pocketed that Pennington used for the corkscrew tool when the real thing wasn't handy and a blade he used for opening mail, he carved a garish gash in her throat stretching from diamond stud to diamond stud.

He left the body in her cute car, then headed for the rearmost, little used entrance, to the mall. If anyone had been paying attention they would have noticed he walked with a slight swagger combined with a guarded peacock gait until he reached the mall and his pace and carriage changed to a mincing step.

Acting like any other shopper, Bad Penny-Pennington admired the windows in the Mont Blanc shop before entering to ogle the expensive fountain pens.

It wasn't long before in what had become a habit, murdering making him hungry, he decided to walk across the street to Houston's, a trendy fern bar and restaurant.

As usual, deciding to sit at the bar to have his lunch, even though it was almost full, he found a seat.

Famous for their club salad with mixed greens, fried chicken bites, avocado, cheese and smoked bacon, he decided on it with vinaigrette dressing.

"Hello," said the woman in business attire next to him.

"How are you?"

"Just fine, thank you. Happy Thanksgiving a few days early."

"Same to you, darling.

Pennington remembered that due to being distracted by Bad Penny's evil needs he'd have to make a return trip to the mall to get Ashley's sweater.

***

"Damn," was the first word Detective Ramsey spoke when he entered the precinct Monday morning.

"What's the problem, partner? Thanksgiving is in three days. It's a short week. We're golden."

"The golden boy always is. The rest of us, not so much."

"What is it?"

Ramsey shrugged off his parka. "The *accident* on Stone Mountain, the girl with her skull caved in in the mountains, and now a dead girl in her car at Lenox. It just smells like Wentworth to me."

"You're shittin' me."

"I shit you not."

"Well, you know if you believe it I do. You want to go pay him a visit? Tune him up?"

"Not yet, partner. It's only been women so far. You remember he was an equal opportunity skel. It made no difference to him, female, male, Asian, white, straight, gay, no difference to Wentworth. Thinking back, I guess the only group not represented was African Americans. Let's see what happens after Thanksgiving."

***

Following Bryan's address from where he entered it on Apple maps on his iPad, Bad Penny/Pennington took Marta to the station closest to his house, then walked three blocks. Couldn't have his car seen at Bryan's house. Or take Uber. They kept records.

He arrived at Bryan's house in the old, but trendier-than-ever Virginia Highlands neighborhood of Atlanta at noon on Thanksgiving Day. A green late model Volkswagon bug eschewing the one car garage, was parked on the short driveway. A cottage that had been completely redone, inside and out. He'd been told to expect dinner at three, but he could arrive early and until then they could nosh on snacks and sip wine and watch football, if he was interested

Bryan greeted Pennington/Bad Penny with a quick peck. With no plans to go outside, he wore khaki colored chinos, a rust and brown-plaid long sleeve cotton Polo dress shirt and brown lace up oxfords. He was a perfect host. His home was warm compared to the outside temps, with a beautiful blazing fire laid in the two-sided fireplace that opened between the family room and the kitchen. Cinnamon scented candles placed around the family room and kitchen gave the room a deliciously Christmas aroma.

"I plan on decorating my trees tomorrow. One in the family room and one out on the deck since it's covered. I hope that doesn't bother you." Even though Bad Penny hadn't particularly noticed it when they met, he now picked up on Bryan's heavy, lucsciously rich, cultured South Carolinian accent. One would think old world Charleston, or even Savannah, GA.

"Of course not. I think if you put up a tree before Thanksgiving you're doing it too early." *And I don't think you'll be putting them up after Thanksgiving, either.*

"I'm going to put the Pinot noir outside on the deck. That will keep it the perfect temperature for dinner." The deck was constructed of a composite material instead of wood, a red, stain-like color and because the cottage had a walkout basement, the surface was a good fifteen feet from the ground, and the railing about nineteen. The backyard was shielded on the three sides that weren't blinded by the house itself by trees shrouded in autumn colors hiding the deck from nosy neighbors.

Pennington then took the bottle of Pinot outside and stood it up in the center of a coil of thick rope left by the workers that had constructed the new deck. The heavy rope gave him an evil idea.

Talking to the open door, Bryan said, "Sounds good, buddy. I have a chard in the fridge that should be ready any minute now."

Bad Penny/Pennington came back in, clapped his mittened hands and said, "Brrr, nice deck. Chard sounds perfect. And I'll put the Rose' in your freezer for a few minutes to get it ready" he said as he walked over to the fridge and pulled open the bottom freezer drawer to lay it on top of a frozen package of ground turkey.

Bryan pulled the dressing out of the oven and replaced it with a sweet potato casserole covered in marshmallows.

"The sweet potatoes are beautiful."

"Thank you. I think you'll like them."

"I know I will."

Bad Penny/Pennington wasn't a football fan, but he sat down on a large sectional in the family room where the widescreen television was tuned to what even he knew was the traditional Thanksgiving day game between the Detroit Lions and somebody else, in today's case, the Green Bay Packers. A classic matchup between NFC Central Division foes.With the game late in the first quarter, Bryan peeked in from the kitchen and said, "You ready for that glass of chard, Francis?"

"Sure, thanks."

"We'll eat about the time the game ends."

"Great."

Bryan returned with a glass for each of them a minute later. "Everything is ready or in the oven, so I'll sit down a minute."

"Please do."

"So, who's playing?"

"The Lions and Packers. It's tradition. The Lions always play on Thanksgiving Day."

"Oh, I didn't know that."

"The only reason I do is because my dad used to make me watch football with him when I was little. Thinking back, I guess maybe he did it because he thought it would keep me from turning out like I did. Well, so much for that." And he tilted the wineglass at Bryan. "But at least I can enjoy football now and know a little bit about it."

"I've traditionally watched the Macy's Thanksgiving Day Parade, then the Westminster Dog Show after."

"Oh, me too. I love dogs."

"So do I. We always had dogs when I was a kid."

At halftime they went out on the deck for a few minutes and Pennington/Bad Penny was able to deflect Bryan's advances without causing him to question his purpose.

Dressed in only a shirt and pants and feeling the chill, Bryan said, "Maybe we should go back in. The second half is starting."

"Whatever you think."

The Pack was kicking off to the Lions.

"So, what are you doing for Christmas," Bryan asked.

"Well, I really don't have any family, except for a friend of mine, Ashley, she's like family. We've been friends since sophomore year of college. So, anyway, nothing special. "Overdose on all the Christmas movies on tv. I love *Home Alone2 Lost In New York.* Midnight Mass on Christmas Eve, probably go to a local hotel for dinner on Christmas Day. How about you?" He needed to steer the conversation away from himself since most of his story was bullshit.

"That's my favorite Christmas movie, too. But, you know how it is. My parents will want me to come back to Columbia for Christmas, but I have zero interest in doing that. They just don't get me."

The Lions scored on a short pass from Matthew Stafford to a backup running back to start the scoring in the second half and go up by four.

With no more scoring half way into the fourth quarter, Francis said, "Wow, what a boring game."

"We can eat now if you'd like. It's ready. All I have to do is put a couple things on the table and...carve the turkey."

"I'm ready if you are."

"Would you mind grabbing that bottle of pinot you put on the deck? That was a good idea, by the way. My fridge is full and it wouldn't have fit, anyway.

"Sure."

Bryan had out done himself. The dining room table looked like the one in the holiday movie, *It's A Wonderful Life*. Only in color, not black and white.

"Would you like to carve the turkey?"

"No, Bryan, your home, your turkey. You carve. It's only right." Truth be told Bad Penny was concerned he might carve it like he were filleting a human body and with a large razor-sharp knife in his hand he might be unable to resist the urge to carve up his host and he really did want a fine dinner before he'd have to leave in a hurry.

Okay, then. What do you like? White or dark meat?"

"A wee bit of both?"

"Certainly."

"I like to have leftovers for turkey salad, sandwiches, and such, so I went a little large on the bird for just two people." It was a beautiful fourteen pound bird.

"What he doesn't know is he'll never get to eat any leftovers. Maybe I should take some home with me."

"Well, Martha must know what she's doing because it's beautiful."

"Thank you."

Bad Penny filled his plate. Not a centimeter of the traditional Thanksgiving motif showed through, covered as it was with turkey, dressing, sweet potatoes, green beans, mashed potatoes, and the sine qua non—cranberry sauce.

Bad Penny opened the bottle of Pinot Noir with a corkscrew Bryan had lain on the table and poured them each a healthy portion.

"Bon Appetito," he said.

"Bon Appetito. Good choice on the wine, by the way."

"Thank you, and everything looks delicious, Bryan. Thank you for inviting me."

"You're most welcome. Thank you for joining me."

Like with most men, while eating there was a lull in the conversation.

Bad Penny-Francis asked for seconds and poured them each a second glass of the delicious red wine.

"I like a man with a healthy appetite."

"You should like me, then." Bad Penny said with a smirk. He was playing a role.

"I do," he said and winked at him.

You think you do.

As Bad Penny-Francis worked on his second plate Bryan began to clear the table.

"Would you like desert, pumpkin pie, or bourbon chocolate?"

"It isn't Thanksgiving without pumpkin pie."

"I agree completely."

"And maybe a glass of cab?"

"We're thinking alike."

Returning from the kitchen with the pie and a bottle of Caymus, Bryan said, "Let's have it in front of the tv." The second game, the Dallas Cowboys hosting their division rival, Washington Redskins, was kicking off.

"Perfect," said Bad Penny.

Biting into the silky smooth pie, and drawing in a mouthful of the expensive Cabernet, Bad Penny said, "I thought you said you weren't much of a baker. This is delicious. And the Caymus is a surprising treat. I went to the winery the last time I was in Napa. It's a beautiful place."

"Thank you. I'm glad you like it. I've always wanted to go to Napa."

"Like it? I love it."

A few bites and it was gone. "Let me take your plate," and Bryan disappeared into the kitchen with nothing but crumbs on their pie plates. When he returned he topped off his guest's glass.

"I'm going to slip into something more comfortable," said Bryan, and he retreated to the rear of the small home.

Five minutes later he returned, more comfortable if he were going to get in the shower, since he was fully nude. He sat down next to Bad Penny, and said, "Join me?"

Bad Penny raised up from the couch and using his body's rising momentum he surprised his host with an uppercut under the chin with his strong right fist, breaking his jaw and breaking or knocking out several teeth and causing him to bite his tongue in two when his upper and lower teeth crashed together. Bryan, unconscious, fell limp into Bad Penny's arms.

Once the opportunity presented itself, he had to move quickly. Gathered up his date's limp form and carried him outside to the cold of the deck. Dropped him on the surface and gathering up the coil of rope, in less than three minutes, fashioned a noose on one end and tied the other end off on the deck's top rail. He then looped the noose over Bryan's still immobile head.

With a chilly wind from the north pummeling him in the face, he pressed the body over his head to the full extension of his arms aiming to get as much height as possible, and threw the inert form toward the flowerbed below. When the rope stretched taut the body continued its descent to land on it's knees in a traditional position of prayer among the peonies until it tottered forward with a torrent of blood exploding from the neck's large orifice. The head took a different path and rolled to a rest in the pansies. If Jacob's ladder had divinely appeared he'd have been unable to ascend it to the deck, much less to Heaven's Gate.

Bad Penny roared in exultation at his artistic annihilation.

The flower bed now had the look of Elysian Fields.

With dusk morphing into dark Bad Penny-Pennington figured he'd be safe walking to the MARTA station and less likely that anyone would notice or remember him.

***

Exhausted physically, and emotionally drained from his Thanksgiving *celebration*, Pennington unintentionally slept in on Black Friday. He had planned on going to the mall again, to lose himself in the crowds, but he was too drained.

After he awoke, at almost noon, he turned on the local midday news and there was no mention of Bad Penny's latest and goriest murder, yet. He had guessed correctly that someone who was new to town with no family nearby and few friends wouldn't be noticed as missing right away.

Friday night came and Pennington went out on the town wishing there were some way he could ditch Bad Penny, or at least control him. Ignorance truly had been bliss when, the year before and Bad Penny made his first appearance, and Pennington never knew he was there.

Chapter Eleven
Out of Control

Monday morning and detectives Ramsey and Townsend arrived at the door to the squadroom at the same time. Townsend said,"Morning, partner, you were right."

"About what? The lottery, Falcons beating the Saints? What?"

"The dead guy who lost his head on Thanksgiving Day."

"Oh, that. Helluva a way to celebrate the holiday. I think he got a little carried away."

"I hear you. Or at least his head did."

"From what I hear, neighbors said he's gay."

"Not that there's anything wrong with that."

"I knew you were going to say that. You know, it's not normal for a brother to be as big a fan of Seinfeld as you are. There's probably no whiter show in the history of television. Except maybe Andy Griffith."

"What, you think I should only watch *Good Times*?"

"I'm just sayin.' "

"I know. I know. You're always just sayin'."

"Well, anyway, Now I'm ready to go tune up Wentworth. That's four now, three women and a gay man, and it's just smelling more and more like him."

"I'm with you, partner. At the worst it can't hurt."

***

They made the fifteen minute drive north on Peachtree Street until they reached the proud highrise. Parked their usual unmarked car in a space with a sign that read Law Enforcement Only.

They badged the concierge. "You need to let us up to Pennington Wentworth's unit."

The director of concierges, a middle eastern immigrant, intimidated by the show of shields, didn't call Pennington to get his permission, which was not the norm, and keyed the elevator for them without hesitation. The detectives didn't want Wentworth to have even one minute to collect his thoughts and think about what to say.

An instrumental version of a Pitbull hip hop song played on the elevator. A minute later they were exiting the elevator onto

Pennington's twenty-fourth floor. Turned to the left and then right to go to the north side of the floor.

"How're we going to play this?" Townsend asked Ramsey.

"Just an interview. Idle curiosity. In fact, I just had an idea. How about we ask him for his his thoughts, ask him for his help, what he thinks, what he would look for. But hint at the idea that we could just as easily like him for it, but subtly. That sort of thing. Maybe he'll get a nervous twitch. Give us a 'tell.'"

"Works for me."

It was just after ten o'clock when they knocked on his door.

The sound of the deadbolt turning. "Detectives..."

He said it calmly, but the shock on his face was the "tell" they hoped for. He looked like he hadn't been up long. His hair was mussed and he had a weekend stubble. Probably hadn't shaved since getting ready for his Thanksgiving date. He was wearing flannel burgundy and gray plaid pajama bottoms and a navy blue t-shirt, with a logo, underneath a bathrobe. Tan suede fleece-lined slippers. Where the bathrobe opened they could make out the letters, ON, but on what? He pulled the robe together, looked down at the cinch around the waist and fiddled with it, aware that he was betraying his nervousness.

With a curt nod of his head, Ramsey said, "Wentworth,"

"Good morning, Pennington," Townsend said warmly. They fell into their roles of good cop-bad cop naturally and with ease from years of practice.

"Come in," he said, his tone less than enthusiastic. He quickly added, "Let me get something else on."

Pennington's iPad sat on the counter where he'd been reading the local news on the *Atlanta Journal and Constitution's* website.

The detectives knew he'd feel even more vulnerable dressed as he was and them dressed for business. He gestured to the shiny red Bosch and Lomb appliance as he walked past it to his private rooms, and said "Help yourself to some coffee. It's Starbucks Dark Roast. I grind it myself every morning. Sugar's in that blue container and creamer's in the fridge door. Mugs are on that shelf," pointing to it. "Don't be shy."

The detectives had little choice but to accede.

Ramsey helped himself. "That's some damn good coffee, partner."

Pennington had been rattled by their arrival, but he'd gotten over it. Of course, he'd been through a lot, including a trial, conviction, prison and death row. It was unlikely they could worry him much, especially since he'd changed out of the STONE MOUNTAIN tee shirt he'd slept in.

Returning from his bedroom, now dressed in a fall-flannel shirt and jeans, he casually darkened his iPad, then, although he almost choked on the words, he said, "There, now I'm proper. What can I do for you gentlemen?"

Townsend began, "First, Pennington, let me apologize for coming to see you without calling first, but we just thought of it and we'd like to see if you can help us.

Ramsey interrupted: "Maybe help is too strong of a word, *get your opinion* might be a better way to put it." They switched roles or maybe they were both playing good cop.

"By all means, what can I do?'

Townsend deferred with a nod to Ramsey, who said, "I'm sure you've heard about the recent rash of deaths in the area. We may be a little premature because we're not even sure they're all murders, and even if they are, if they're related. But we were hoping to get your thoughts on it."

"I've heard about them on the news, but it's not like I've really been keeping up with it. And to be honest I don't know how I can help because fortunately all that's behind me, but I'm certainly willing to give it a try. "

"Thank you, Pennington. You know, we knew all along you were really a good guy and just a victim of circumstances." They knew they were blowing some serious smoke up his ass. They just hoped he wouldn't figure that out. "So that's all we're asking."

They are blowing some serious smoke up my ass. They must really need help.

"Don't trust these guys. They're worse than we are. What douchebags. "

I wondered when you were going to show up.

"Dude, I'm here for you. Don't worry about it. We can handle this. "

They sat at his glass-topped breakfast table looking down on Atlanta's Broadway—Peachtree Street.

"Nice view," said Townsend.

"Thanks. Is the coffee okay?"

"Excellent," said Townsend, while Ramsey was succinct and to the point.

"That's a damn fine cuppa Joe,"

"Funny, because it's Jittery Joe's from Alon's. So, where do we start? Excuse me, where are my manners? Would you like a bagel?"

"No thanks."

"Not for me."

"Do you mind if I have one?"

"Go right ahead."

Pennington stepped to a cabinet and retrieved a package of whole grain bagels, then moseyed to the refrigerator and got a butter dish and a small jar of black cherry preserves. Selected a serrated bread knife and a condiments spoon from a drawer. Before sitting down he sawed the bagel in two on a Georgia-shaped cutting board and put each piece into the dual slots of a red Bausch and Lomb toaster that matched his coffee maker. It would be obvious to anyone that everything about Pennington's image, from his clothes, to his condo, furniture and accessories filling it, was carefully crafted. He's a vain young man and cared deeply about his presentation in everything he did.

While Pennington stood waiting for the bagel to brown Ramsey asked, "What do you think the common thread between the victims is?" Ramsey's idea. His interview.

"This is just a guess, mind you. But I don't see a thread. They're crimes of opportunity."

"Good, don't even hint at the dating sites, straight or gay. We'll use them again."

I want to return to prison even less than you do. You can handle it. I can't. And contrary to what you think, I'm the more intelligent one of us, so let me take care of this part. If you can just resist your sick urges we'll get through this.

"Showing a little backbone. I like that. Just remember who's in charge."

"If they are connected, then where do you think he's finding them?"

"Anywhere. The supermarket, fast food restaurants, the mall."

They continued for the better part of an hour, the detectives trying to box in Pennington and Pennington refusing to be boxed in.

Townsend offered his hand, said, "Thank you, Pennington."

"You're very welcome, but I don't think anything I said was very enlightening."

"Well, you never know. We're just beginning to work all the angles and you gave us some things to think about."

Back in the elevator, Townsend asked, "So, what do you think, partner?"

"I think that they are related and I believe that we were looking into the soulless eyes of the killer." He's smooth, but I believe he's our man."

"So, what next?"

"I think, since we're dealing with two in the ATL, one in Stone Mountain and one in Lumpkin County, I think we should get Lou to go to bat for us with the captain and put together a multi-jurisdictional task force. And since, so far we have two in our jurisdiction and only one in two others and, our experience with Wentworth, I think you and I should head it up."

"I think that sounds like a plan, partner. Let's go see Lou soon as we get back and make it happen."

"Dude, I have to admit you handled that very well. Leading them in other directions was a stroke of genius."

Well, like I told you, you may be the brawn, but I'm definitely the brains.

"Now, don't get carried away."

***

"So, let me see if I understand this. You think they're all homicides, including the one that fell off Stone Mountain, and you think they're related *and* you think Wentworth committed these murders and you want me to get the captain's approval for this...this multi-jurisdictional task force, you called it, with not one stitch of evidence. Your hunch only. Townsend, Ramsey's been doing all the talking; you haven't said anything. Is the golden boy onboard with this?

"Yeah, Lou. I am."

"Sorry Nick. I had to ask. You know how you get...allright then, if the golden boy agrees, I'll do it."

"Thanks, Lou. And by the way. It's not just a hunch. It's intuition, honed by experience...and knowing Wentworth." Ramsey's feelings were a little hurt by what the lieutenant had said.

"Whatever you call it, just stop him before there are anymore killings."

"Yeah, thanks Lou. We'll do our best." Townsend knew that short of locking him up and throwing away the key, there'd be no way to stop him if he wanted to kill again.

***

After the detectives left, Pennington decided to check the dating websites for nibbles.

"Good idea. Alternate between the gay and straight site. If they get the idea and go looking we don't want them to notice a pattern."

Look, dammit, I hope to find someone I like. I'm not looking for your next victim.

"Just remember. Those things aren't necessarily mutually exclusive."

Well, they need to be.

"I've warned you about getting too froggy with me. You need to just relax and enjoy it."

As it turned out, Pennington'd had a half a dozen women contact him on the straight website over the weekend. All but one had been his type, brunettes, cute, educated. The other had been a blonde, which he wouldn't completely discount, but still not his favorite. He responded to the others with faves, likes or flirts. Canned responses that didn't take long, so he wouldn't waste time, in case they didn't amount to anything. Then he waited.

He didn't have to wait long. Two replied within an hour with their names and asking questions about him.

He spent the rest of the afternoon going back and forth with both, being clever and charming.

A third girl contacted him a couple of hours later and he began to realize just why online dating was storming the country.

Starting Monday he spent a couple days chatting with them online, then asked Jane, no last name, since no one gave their last names on dating sites, until after meeting, and the one he thought was the cutest, if she wanted to meet for a glass of wine Thursday.

She eagerly accepted and they agreed to meet at Seasons 52 in

Dunwoody, one of a nationwide chain of about seventy restaurants, and one of a pair in Atlanta, in mostly larger cities across the country.

December arrived, Thursday rolled around, and as someone who'd always loved Christmas, Pennington was even more excited than usual to meet a new girl at the beginning of the holiday season. The classy restaurant was across the street from Perimeter Mall, one of Atlanta's premier shopping and entertainment destinations.

While he was getting dressed, Bad Penny made his presence known.

"The weather report said there's a full moon tonight. You know how they say a full moon affects behavior, people and animals, more babies are conceived, more crimes are committed, etc? I wonder what effect it's going to have on me. Heh, heh, heh."

I'm not paying attention to you. I'm ignoring you.

Loud even inside on his penthouse level, police sirens caused Pennington's heart rate to elevate. Looking out a window he saw two cop cars had a yellow SUV pulled over on traffic-clogged Peachtree Street, twenty-four floors below, so he relaxed, knowing they weren't coming for him.

While dressing he noticed he was getting low on his favorite cologne, Tom Ford Tobacco Vanille, so on the way to meet his date, he stopped by Nordstrom's at Perimeter Mall to pick up a bottle of the expensive mens' fragrance. Couldn't afford to run out of his signature scent.

As he entered the mens' fragrance department a super cute young Chinese woman approached him. "How can I help you?"

"I need some Tom Ford Tobacco Vanille."

"I thought you looked like a Tom Ford man." She said, subtly flirting with him.

"Thank you. I hope so."

"She likes us. If our date doesn't work out. We can come back here at closing."

She doesn't like us. She likes me. And we don't have a date. I do.

"My, my, my, aren't we touchy tonight?"

He paid for the purchase with his AmEx Black Card and the young woman's eyes got big. Depending on how long she'd worked there, there was a good chance she'd never seen one.

Pennington exited the parking lot to the street circling the mall and it was no more than three hundred yards to the rendezvous spot. They agreed to meet at seven but he told her he'd arrive before her, so she'd know he was there.

Entering the restaurant, T.J., according to the gold name tag he wore, a handsome young man with a neatly sculpted beard, led him past an invitingly warm glass-front fireplace on his right, and to the left, a dining room nearly full of people enjoying their dinners and lively conversations, and escorted him to a huge bar full of sophisticated men and women, and secured for him a prime seat. Pennington had told Jane he'd be sitting at the bar.

Pennington had only been to Seasons 52 one time before but was surprised to see they'd removed the piano from the center of the bar, where different musicians played and sang seven nights a week. The blonde wood floors were new and looked good with the red leather bar stools. Stacked stone walls gave the room a warm, cozy, comfortable ambiance.

A good crowd on a Thursday, full of people streaming in from the many nearby office buildings for after work happy hour, he sat in one of the only pair of barstools. Pennington could smell the sexual tension mixed with the different colognes and perfumes of the good looking, well dressed people trying to hookup with someone to make the holidays a little less lonely.

Sitting at the front end of the bar where Jane would easily spot him, he'd described to her how he'd be dressed in his usual designer jeans, and an olive green, wool, houndstooth sport coat with brown felt elbow patches, over a white open collar dress shirt. He'd told her to look for an adjunct college professor,

In the middle of a business community with several hotels within walking distance, there were quite a few business travelers, domestic and international, enjoying the well-known national chain restaurant. The man sitting nearest to his right was speaking with an Israeli accent. The white shirt he wore with a tie was wilted from a long day of work. But he had great hair. Dark, with a hint of gray at the temple, below his collar and pulled back behind his ears. Probably an engineer—a high technology support person.

The bartender, an African-American man who appeared to be in his mid-to-late thirties, with a shiny, black shaved head and off the chain personality, said, "Hey brother. My name's Gerald." He extended his hand. "You also have De Angelo, Anguelo and Mel behind the bar. You flying solo or you expecting someone? You dining with me or just getting drinks?"

"I'm Francis. I'm expecting someone. We'll probably eat here at the bar, but, in the meantime I'll have a house Chardonnay."

"Nice to meet you, Francis. You got it. What do you like? Heavy oak, butter, or steel aged?" And he shook hands again.

"Cut down an oak tree and put about a pound of butter in it."

Seasons 52 was known for having one of the best national chain wine lists in the nation. He knew the chard would be excellent, whatever it was.

Pouring Pennington the glass of white wine and delivering two placemats and silverware, Gerald said, "I think you'll like this chard. It's bold but approachable. Let me set you up for success." He scanned the bar using his hand like a football player counting his teammates to ensure they had enough players on the field to confirm to himself that everyone in his domain had been taken care of.

Pennington could tell he'd repeated those lines thousands of times, but it didn't matter. Gerald made you feel like you were the only customer he'd ever served. And, you were his best friend.

Half way finished with the first glass, a pretty young woman approached. She was dressed in a curves hugging dress of autumn colors—sunset, ochre and gold. Pennington thought it looked like Century 21. As she came closer he could see that her eyes were the color of country French blue willow china. She was of average size body, but with an ample chest, which Pennington liked.

"Francis?"

"Yes. Jane?" She nodded. "Nice to meet you."

"Nice to meet you."

"She's a hottie."

Shut up and just do something else.

"This is a lovely place. I'm glad you suggested it." *Just Give Me A Reason* by Pink and Nate Ruess came forth from speakers above their heads.

"Thanks." He glanced around. "I'm glad you accepted. I haven't been here in a long time and I'd forgotten just how nice it is. It looks like they've remodeled since I was here, though."

Stacked stone walls were on one side of the bar. Booths circled it and small, romantic red-shade lamps were spaced every few feet on the redwood bartop.

"What would you like to drink?

"What are you having?

"A Chardonnay."

"That sounds good."

"Gerald, can we have another chard for the lady? And maybe you could hit me again. And we'd like to order some food."

"You got it, my friend."

"I assume you'd like something to eat."

"To be honest, I didn't think I was hungry until I got here. But it smells so good, I have to admit I could eat something now."

"Great, Shall we share a pepperoni flatbread? Do you eat pepperoni? Do you mind if we do gluten free? Is that okay?"

"That sounds perfect."

Gerald brought over their glasses of wine, took their food order and the wine began to loosen their tongues.

"So, where are you from, Jane?"

"I'm a rare bird, a native of the ATL. What about you?"

Not so rare, I am too. But he thought it best to stick to his newest contrived background. "Northern Virginia, DC burbs, James Madison University, U.S. History major." It was easier to keep things straight and not mess up if he kept to the same story. "Happy to be in the real south instead of up where they *think* it's the south." He rubbed his cheek as he talked, pleased with the smooth shave he'd gotten right before he left home.

"This *is* the storied old money south, isn't it? She took a healthy sip from her glass. "And this is excellent Chardonnay."

If she only knew. His old family money would blow her mind And now it was his…all his.

Gerald set the flatbread on the bar between them. It didn't take long due to it being one of their most popular dishes and they always had it ready to go. There were two others nearby having the same dish.

"Yes, it is."

"Do you like Christmas?" She asked as she extracted a triangle. Melted cheese strung from her slice to the rest. He covered her free hand with his as he looked deep into her eyes.

"Are you kidding me? I live for Christmas. I'll be decorating my trees this weekend and can't wait for it to get here. The food, the music, decorations, the smells. All of it. In fact if it were up to me, they would be playing Christmas music right now."

"You sound just like me." She leaned close and placed her hand on his thigh and gave it a familiar squeeze, as she tried to find things they had in common.

After finishing her glass, and her first bite of flatbread, she dabbed her mouth daintily and said, "I need to go to the restroom. Do you know where it is?"

"In the left hand corner, past the front door to the left," he said as he subtly pointed toward the entrance, so as not to embarrass her.

"Be right back,"she said as she waggled two fingers at him from a place next to her face while she rose from the red leather barstool and turned toward the front.

He watched her walk away. If anyone had been paying attention, or cared, they would have thought he was leering too intently. But everyone was involved in their own dates, or the person they hoped would be their next date, or their cocktails.

"Dude, she has a butt to die for; no pun intended. And she likes us. So, we won't kill her...yet."

And I told you, she likes me. And we won't kill her ever.

"Whatev."

Whatev? You too lazy to use full words?

"Don't push me."

"Miss me?"when she returned.

"You know I did, but I have a confession to make."

"Okaay." She wondered what could be so serious.

But, with a bad boy grin on his face, he said, "When you walked away I watched your butt until you were out of sight."

"Oh, that. I hope so. We women have to pretend we don't like it, but we really want you to notice. But you're the first man who's ever told me he was staring."

"I think it's best to be honest."

Jane playfully punched him on his arm. "You're bad."

"You know it, baby."

They each had another glass of wine, finished the flatbread, and made small talk. Jane worked for a local insurance company. *Shoot me now,* Bad Penny thought. He continued with his new story of having just come back to town, was looking for a job, but this time as an HR specialist. *Thank God that's bullshit.*

After enough time to show that she was interested and not be rude, she said, "Well, I probably should call it a night. Six o'clock comes pretty early on a Friday morning." Jane was serious about her career and wouldn't be late or go in with a hangover.

Double teaming them for the best possible service, a different bartender, De Angelo, a tall, handsome African-American with another perfectly shaved and shiny head, came over. "Do y'all need dessert?"

"I don't think so. Can I have my check?"

"Coming up."

He gave DeAngelo cash since "Francis" didn't want anyone to notice that his American Express said PENNINGTON WENTWORTH, and besides he didn't want to leave a record of having been there in case anyone did recall Jane being there with some dude named "Francis."

"I'll see you to your car."

"Thank you. A woman shouldn't walk through a dark parking lot alone in this day and time."

"I'll need to go to the restroom before we leave; if you don't mind."

"Of course not. I'll go, too."

As they exited the fashionable restaurant, a cold and bitter December north wind blasted them in the face taking their breath away.

No one was entering at the late hour and most of the cars in the nearly empty parking lot belonged to workers.

"I just noticed you have a slight limp. What happened?"

He grinned and said, "I was competing in the Joust, and the Black Knight, nasty bugger, dislodged me from my steed. Bloody knee hasn't been the same since." Jane guessed he'd rehearsed—and delivered— that clever story more than a few times. She grinned and raised an eyebrow with appreciation in an attempt to encourage him to tell her the real one. He didn't offer so she didn't question further.

As they walked, Bad Penny surreptitiously checked out the building corners, and parking lot light poles. Although video cameras were usually everywhere in big cities—big brother's eye watching everything we do—he didn't see any. It appeared that the Dunwoody neighborhood was more trusting than the large metropolis that was Atlanta. The temperature had dropped since they entered the popular restaurant. Jane shivered and Pennington took off his stylish wool sport coat and wrapped it around her shoulders. "Thank you," she said. "Gentlemen are rare these days." As they approached a newish white Toyota Camry, she asked, "Where is your car?"

A lie, but Bad Penny told her, "I took Uber tonight." Fortunately for him, he'd parked across the street from the restaurant in the Perimeter Mall parking lot so even if he were late returning, the car wouldn't draw a lot of attention. He wasn't worried about the bartender remembering him if anyone tied her to the restaurant. He'd used a fake name and knew that in most cases, five different people would give law enforcement five different descriptions of the same person.

"Why don't I drive you home?"

"That would be nice, but are you sure? You don't really know me."

"I'm a pretty good judge of people."

"A lady shouldn't take chances, though. But alrighty then."

"Good, it's all settled."

She got behind the wheel of the family-style sedan and popped the automatic lock release to let him in the passenger side door.

He slipped in and said, "Ready when you are."

"Buckle up for safety." She smiled provocatively

Her tight dress inched up her leg with every movement she made revealing an attractive expanse of white upper thigh.

She reached to turn on the radio. "What kind of music do you like?"

"Almost all current music. Bruno Mars, Fun., Ed Sheeran, Justin Bieber."

"Me, too. Those're all good ones."

He gave her directions to his Buckhead condo remembering to tell her which turns to make, but just before going over I-285 to get inside the perimeter, he surprised her by saying, "Pull in here." It was a dark parking lot on Roswell Road. She did as she was told when he told her to pull up at the end of a run down, late twentieth century strip center. A liquor store was dark and empty having closed an hour before. The rest of the businesses had closed years before.

As he leaned toward her he said, "I'm sorry I couldn't wait any longer. I'm sorry. I just had to kiss you now."

"Then why didn't you just say so? You didn't have to resort to games."

Bad Penny closed his eyes; she closed hers, even in the dark better for her not to see, the glint of the blade hidden beneath his knee.

As he moved in for the kiss, the kiss of death? He buried the short fixed knife into her abdomen, and as he ripped it upward, her eyes opened with shock and a violent gasp escaped the gash of her mouth as it tore through her sternum ripping her rib cage apart. The hot blood of life landed on his hand and wrist before turning cold in the frigid December air.

Pennington began to sob, sickened by the salty metallic smell of the stickiness. He opened a window so the fresh air would keep him from getting sick. As he sat there trying to recover from Bad Penny's terror, he formulated his escape plan. He then used a tissue he found in a package on the backseat to wipe down everything he'd touched, mainly the passenger side door handle and the seatbelt latch.

After deciding on a plan, he made his way through a quarter mile of wooded undergrowth toward I-285. He could hear the traffic and see light through the skeletons of tree trunks. The different tree's leaves were all turning a similar shade of brown, no matter their species, if any foliage at all still clung at the beginning of December. In the dark he stepped gingerly, a crunch from the quilt of fallen leaves accompanying his every step. He hesitated, surveying the scene and crouched at the edge of the copse. He could see the white of his breath from the cold exertion of getting through the trees. Then he scrambled, in a crouch, up the incline of open ground to the highway shoulder. The organic musty smell of the Chattahoochee River mixed with car exhaust wafted on the dark night air.

Real casual like, he stuck out his thumb, trying to appear to passing traffic like he'd been on the shoulder for awhile instead of just emerging from the trees. The flow of vehicles was unexceptional at eleven pm on a Thursday night in one of the busiest cities in the world for traffic. Even at the start of the Christmas season. Not heavy; not light. Illuminated in the beam of headlights and being fairly well dressed, he hoped someone would take pity on him soon.

A twenty minute wait, and an expensive metallic gray Lexus sedan pulled to the shoulder, a middle-aged man, not younger than forty-five, nor older than fifty, in dark pants, white shirt and red power tie, fingered the button to power down the window and leaned over to look under the door jamb before popping the door lock to allow him entry.

He moved his suit coat from the passenger seat to twist around and lay it on the rear seat.

"Hop in. where do you need to go?"

"My car broke down at Perimeter Mall...outside Dillard's." Although he'd cleaned the blood from his skin with the tissue he'd used to wipe down Jane's car's surfaces he'd touched, he hoped the man woudn't smell the acrid odor of death on him.

"That's not too far driving, but it's pretty far to walk on a cold night. And you aren't exactly dressed for it. How'd you get here?"

So, he thought of the story he concocted on his stroll through the woods and figured it had better be good.

"I'm Francis, by the way. I work at the mall, you know the mens' department at Dillard's. You should come see me sometime. I'll hook you up. Anyway, when I got off after closing at ten; I hate closing; It takes forever to reconcile those damn registers, I went out to my car and it just wouldn't start. I figure it's the battery. I'm pretty good around an engine, you know. And I'm standing there with the hood up looking at it and this guy pulls up and offers me a ride. Usually I wouldn't take a chance like that, but he's in a nice car, a new Honda, so I figure what the hell, so I say okay, and I swear if I'm lying I'm dying, as soon as I got in I got the heebie jeebies, the guy just had the look and smell of a serial killer and when we pulled up at that red light back there at the entrance ramp, I just jumped out and started running. And that's how I got here."

"So, why didn't you just call somebody to come get you?"

"Well, I accidentally left my darn phone in the car. I'm getting bad about that lately, and besides I just moved here, back on Labor Day weekend, you know, so I really don't know many people. So I'm really glad you came along when you did."

"Well, I'm glad I did too. But what are you going to do about getting it started?

"Like I said, I'm pretty good with cars so given some time, I'm pretty sure I can get it going. My old man was a mechanic. I take after him. I should've just kept at it til I got it going."

"Well, I'll wait with you just to make sure."

"That's very generous of you. I would be grateful, if you did; Just til I get it started, you know. That parking lot will be deserted at this time of night."

From Ashford-Dunwoody Road, Pennington directed him to enter the main drive to the mall parking lot then drive around to the right to one of the two side entrances of Dillard's.

"There it is." He pointed out the sensible gold Toyota Prius that he liked so much.

Pennington hopped out and said, "Let me try it again first." He knew it would start immediately, so he just bumped the ignition two quick times, faking a problem, before holding it down to make it engage. He gave his "savior" a grin and a thumbs up through the window.

Then he got out, walked over to the man's driver side window and thanked him. "What's your name, by the way?"

"Harvey, Harvey Walker. Here's my card." Pennington held it in both hands to study it under the parking lot lights. It read "HARVEY WALKER SENIOR ACCOUNT MANAGER" in raised shiny formal black print on a stark white linen blend paper. *Very expensive.*

Harvey saw the puzzled look on Pennington's face and said, "Technology sales, boring as shit. But it's a living."

"Well, thanks again, Harvey. I really appreciate it a lot. Merry Christmas." Pennington extended his arm toward the window offering his hand. The man shook it. The hand wasn't rough or soft. Maybe the hand of a man who doesn't do manual labor, but has gripped a barbell in his life.

"Glad I could help. You too. Take care." And he drove off.

"Well, Harv ole buddy, you dodged a bullet, though not literally, because I never use a firearm. You don't know how lucky you are, my friend. If my bloodlust hadn't just been sated, you'd be tied to a large stone and on the bottom of the hooch by now."

Pennington tuned his XM Radio to an all-Christmas music station that was playing twenty-four hour a day seasonal music through December twenty-fifth.

"That's nice. I like Christmas music."

Hah, what the hell do you know about Christmas? You're a trip. Celebrating Christ's birth, the Reason for the Season, loving all people? You just killed an innocent young woman in cold blood.

"I think it was us who killed her, buster."

Yeah, but I'm the only one clever enough to keep us out of jail.

The first song he heard was one of his favorite non-traditional

Christmas tunes. *Santa Claus is Coming to Town* by Bruce Springsteen and The E Street Band. It perked up Pennington even after the night's terrible outcome.

He made it home and exhausted mentally and physically from the killing, his trek through the woods and having to "perform" for Harvey, he was too tired to sleep. He poured a glass of Far Niente chardonnay and went out on his terrace to decompress. He was happy to see that Northside Hospital had put their giant lighted Christmas tree on the roof. He considered it his tree since he had such a great view of it from his living room. But he also could see, at a distance, and liked, the lighted tree atop Stone Mountain, which had not been there on his recent excursion to the summit that resulted in such mayhem.

One glass turned into two but he decided to have the second inside and *Home Alone 2, Lost in New York*, his favorite Christmas movie, was on tv, so all he did was crash on the sofa and enjoy it while sipping his last glass of the night.

***

After his late night, Pennington's body decided that it needed to sleep in. He arose around ten and after a cup of coffee—he needed the caffeine—and desiring to not be too libertine, he went down to the lobby gym to get a workout.

First thing he noticed was that since the last time he'd been in the week before, a heavy bag had been hung. And since it was new and the bag gloves hanging on a metal tree were, too, they wouldn't even be that gross. He picked out a pair of red ones and checked the fit. Starting first with his left side forward, threw left jabs, peppering the bag, follow by right crosses, then left hooks to the body, and then the head. Then, switching sides, he rained down hell on the bag with a multitude of right jabs, followed by left crosses, then right hooks to the body then head. Fifteen minutes later sweat was pouring off him, soaking the floor; he was breathing heavy and had gotten in an intense cardio workout.

He then went to the dip-stand and knocked out a set of fifty, and then strutted over—just in case anybody was watching—to his nemesis, the pull-up bar.Though barely able to jump and reach the bar, he powered through a set of twenty-five while changing his grip from palms toward him, to palms facing each other, to mixed grip, with one palm toward him and the other facing his other hand. His biceps were spent.

"You're getting pretty good at those."

Shut up.

***

"God dammit." Ramsey was a man of few words.

"I know," said Townsend. He didn't even have to ask why his partner was swearing.

"Can you believe it? Another dead girl."

'It's a good thing our task force is having its first meeting this morning."

"Yeah, no kidding. We've got to get this thing kicked off."

Once the lieutenant gained agreement from the captain and contacted the various agencies that had had questionable deaths, each department had jumped at the chance to get a possible serial killer off the street.

Stone Mountain Police Department homicide detective Evan Tirk was the first to arrive.

Unusual for a detective, he was dressed to impress, attired as he was in a well-fitting, crisply ironed police department uniform that most, who worked in plain clothes, reserved for special events. He was old school; he wore what was called in today's military or law enforcement, a high-and-tight. In the 60's it would have been known as a flat top.

Tirk was directed to the conference room Townsend and Ramsey had secured for the first meeting of the multi-jurisdictional task force. Apparently it was used when ATL police had to meet with city muckety-mucks since the eight chairs circling the oblong-shaped table were black leather ergonomically designed highback chairs with pneumatic pumps for lowering and raising, and tilt and rotation. They could tell it hadn't been used much since it didn't have the stale, squalid scent of nearly all other meeting rooms in the building. Tirk and Townsend got reaquainted and he and Ramsey exchanged greetings and hands were shook. Next, another APD detective, a young African-American, Cassius Wheeling, which he pronounced properly, the

Roman way, Ca-see-us, just promoted, who they hadn't as yet, had met. Cassius was dark black and so lean his cheekbones pushed out of his face. Looked like he might be part American Indian.

Because of the longest drive, the last to arrive was Steven Lee, the Chief Investigator of the Lumpkin County Sherriff's Department. But Chief Investigator Lee made it clear to everybody they should call him "Bubba." Perps called him either "Mr. Bubba" or "Big Bubba."

Bubba was six-feet-three, two hundred fifty pounds and although he received a scholarship offer from his homestate, University of Georgia Bulldogs, he followed his childhood dream to Alabama where he started at strongside linebacker, becoming an All-American on the Crimson Tide's 2009 National Championship team. Earned his degree in Criminal Justice then returned home to Dahlonega, GA to start his career in law enforcement. At thirty years old he looked like he could still play linebacker.

Although Ramsey was the senior detective, Townsend conducted the meeting because he was the more detailed of the pair. Giving everyone handouts and following an outline projected from his iPad, he listed the murders and the one suspicious death on Stone Mountain and told them how he and his partner had a sense that they were all connected, then told the team how they suspected Wentworth and told them the details about his murders—different races, different sexes, different sexual persuasions, and even a Catholic High Priest—the different weapons of opportunity he used and how his release from prison was secured with help from the Governor, all reasons for suspecting him now.

"A new wrinkle, though," Ramsey said. "The name Francis has been mentioned by witnesses."

"Maybe we're, as you white folks would say," Townsend said, "We're barking up the wrong tree."

"Nah, Wentworth is smart enough to use an alias," Ramsey said, "and not dumb enough to use his real name this time around."

Wrapping up about one o'clock, they all agreed to a late lunch at Fat Mac's Rib Shack. It wasn't hard for them to agree on a place. What most people don't know is cops-and-barbecue go together just about as well as cops-and-donuts.

Everybody took their own cars to the Piedmont Avenue midtown location so they could all go back to their own precinct, county or town.

Even though they were after the traditional lunch hour, the line was still out the door. A smoky sweet smell engulfed them from the open door. Standing in line in the chilly gray weather, A gloveless Tirk blew into his hands to warm them. each of the others rubbed their palms together, or clapped their hands trying to ward off the cold. The wind picked up and each pulled the necks of their jackets together.

"What good is being a cop if you got to wait in line in the cold?" Asked Ramsey of no one.

"Damn straight," said Bubba, the Lumpkin County Chief Investigator, "but it's colder up in the mountains, in my neck of the woods. Just be glad you're not up there."

"I am."

Townsend said, "Feels like we're going to get an early snow this year. A white Christmas sure would be nice."

Bubba said, "You can have it. I bet it's already snowing up in my mountains. Damn! It'll take me even longer to get home."

Once inside they had to wait to get a round table big enough to accommodate five—except for Ramsey—larger than average men, comfortably. It was soon covered with dishes breathing off the delicious aromas of barbecue drenched in their chosen sauces, Memphis or North Carolina style, hot or sweet. Being on duty, they all eschewed beer however, and since this was still the south, they all opted for the most ginormous glasses of sweet tea you've ever seen. And the waitress, a middle aged white woman with brown hair turning to gray, her sweet perfume stifling, brought them three huge pitchers so they could refill their glasses whenever they wanted.

Above the noise of the crowded restaurant, Townsend said, "So what, did you all just guess the brothers would want barbecue? And do y'all figure we eat chitlins, too?" Everybody roared. What made it funny was apparently Townsend had forgotten that he'd been the first one to suggest barbecue.

In addition to their plates of barbecue—pork, chicken and brisket, they ordered large bowls of baked beans, cole slaw, Mac and cheese and Brunswick stew, for sharing family style. Townsend tried to order a bowl of collards but he was quickly overruled by the others.

Over the din—their own and everybody else's—they outlined a game plan. The ATL detectives, Townsend, Ramsey and the new guy, Cassius, would stake out Wentworth's condo, staying visible, in an attempt, if he was the killer, to be a deterrent, at least until they could put together enough hard evidence to arrest him. Of course, if they needed to, they knew that tailing him, in Atlanta traffic, could be at best, problematic, and at worst, damn near impossible. If they knew or had reason to believe he was leaving Fulton County, they would get the others involved depending on the county, city or jurisdiction.

"Damn, that's good barbecue," said Bubba.

"That's for sure," echoed Tirk.

Ramsey said, "If you guys got to the big city more often, we could hit other places just as good."

Chapter Twelve
Mayhem Continues

Pennington decided, with the intention of keeping Bad Penny under control, that he would spend the weekend decorating his condo for the holidays, rather than going out. First weekend in December and he thought he was almost late with so many homes already ablaze with lights and decorated trees all over the city.

He found his iPod that he'd loaded with holiday music a few Christmases before and played it the entire time he was decorating. His living room tree was a nine footer, he lighted with a string of lights of all the colors of the rainbow and blanketed in handmade, old world glass ornaments designed by Christopher Radko. He put a second tree outside on the terrace with all white lights and shiny plastic all-weather ornaments in bright colors.

The finishing touch was red berry wreaths from Restoration Hardware hung on two walls unadorned with artwork and Christopher Radko Christmas cookie jars placed strategically around the living, kitchen, and dining room. By Sunday night all was done

***

Pennington had heard that Johnny's Hideaway, not far away on Roswell Road was a cool place but his parents had liked it when he was a toddler, so he had his doubts, but Wednesday the following week, late in the first week of December, his curiosity got the best of him.

He withdrew the Christmas iPod from where it sat in Ashley's Sounddock to put in his car so he'd have mobile Christmas music during the season. Before going out, on a lark, he put a blonde-colored rinse on his hair that he'd bought long before and chickened out before using.

Although disguise hadn't been Pennington's reason for doing it, on watch alone from his car, Detective Cassius Wheeling failed to recognize the now blonde Wentworth when he exited his building. A few minutes later seeing the Prius now not in its place, he knew his target had somehow, intentionally or unintentionally given him the slip.

Decked out in his best dressed-to-impress cold weather outfit, he pulled into the strip center with Johnny's Hideaway on the north end.

Since the other businesses closed at night, most of the parking lot was designated for Johnny's valet parking. So, he let the valets on duty park his Prius.

Entering, it was so dark Pennington had to give his eyes time to adjust before venturing past the coat room and the greeter's stand.

The first bar was on the left perched across from a small dance floor and the bandstand on the right. Past the bar on the left was a second.

Pennington took a seat—the middle one of three empty seats so he wouldn't crowd anyone on the back side of the first bar so he could face the dance floor without turning around.

He was pleased with the prime location. Observing the crowd he guessed that he was about in the middle, age-wise.

A half an hour later, "Excuse me. Is anyone sitting here?" Said a woman at least thirty years his senior, gesturing toward the barstool to his left.

"No. You're welcome to it if you'd like."

"Well, thank you."

"You're very welcome."

She had bleached blonde hair but she was close to seventy and her breasts were as large as the last woman to sing in an opera. She was probably a knockout when she was young. But that was a long time ago. If he were drunk and very hard up, he might not have minded getting his hands on her boobs but he wasn't that hard up or drunk, yet.

"I haven't seen you here before."

"That's because I haven't been here before. And I infer from that comment that you must be a regular or you wouldn't know that I'm not."

"Got me! Yes, I'm kind of a regular. It's the only place in town that plays Sinatra or Tony."

A four piece band was setting up its equipment on the small stage. Keyboards, lead guitar, bass and drums. The standard set up of most bands for at least forty years.

"I'm Millie," she said, and offered her hand.

"Francis." He might as well go with what had been working for him. Whether or not Bad Penny raised his ugly head, too many people would remember his name and it was best not to bring up that red flag.

"I love that name, Francis. What do you do?"

"I'm in grad school at Georgia Tech."

"Oh, nice. What discipline?"

"IT."

"That will probably be a lucrative field for you. I'm retired, myself. My late husband, God bless him, left me pretty well set."

"That's good for you."

She smiled. The band started it's first number, an old standard by Andy Williams. "Ask a lady to dance?"

"I'm sorry. I really can't. Knee injury." He rubbed his left knee as he said it. He really didn't want to hurt her feelings. She seemed insecure. "I just came to listen to the music."

"Ditch this broad. She actually thinks she has a chance with us."

You, shut up. I'll take care of this.

After a set of everything from Sinatra to Steely Dan the band took a break and Pennington-Francis had had enough. Johnny's was not his style, and he decided to call it a night.

"It was nice to meet you, Millie. I'm going to go to the restroom then be on my way."

"Nice to meet you too, Francis."

The restroom was just down a hallway past the second bar in the back. He saw as he walked by on his way out Millie had departed ahead of him.

When he got outside she was standing on the sidewalk, and as he strolled to his nearby car she called, "Excuse me, Francis. I'm at the the other end of the parking lot. Would you mind terribly shuttling me to my car?"

"Are you sure? You don't know me."

I can tell you're a good person and I know you wouldn't do anything wrong.

The valets had shut down for the evening and so he retrieved his keys from a box and got his own car.

"All right then. I'd be happy to. Come on."

He hit the button on the keyfob to unlock both doors. "Hop in."

They climbed in at the same time and as he put the key in the ignition and before he could start the car, with a coy smile, she said, "I saw you staring at my breasts" and she started pulling the neckline of her top below her massive chest.

"I think you got me wrong. I wasn't staring."

Millie reached over and pulled his face down into the cleavage between the two mounds. He gave each of them a hesitant kiss and said, "Let's at least move further away from the entrance," trying to buy some time to think before he did anything he'd regret.

Then Pennington-Francis said,"Where's your car? I'll move over there."

She pointed to a large several year old burgundy Buick at the other end of the small center. *Why do old people drive Buicks?*

He crept slowly through the parking lot. Francis-Pennington parked the Prius on the other side of Millie's land yacht.

If there had been more light she would have noticed an evil look slowly overtaking his previously peaceful face. Bad Penny was more interested in her than Francis-Pennington had been and after shutting off the engine he leaned over to kiss her and fondle her still exposed breasts. And, while caressing her with one hand he moved his other down to her white neck and encircled it tighter and tighter until he choked the last life giving breath from her lungs. A momentary look of shock registered in her eyes as she came to the realization of what was happening, but both fortunately and unfortunately, it didn't last long,

Now, what to do with the body. Bad Penny shoved the inert form into the passenger seat floorboard and covered it with a jacket he'd left in the car in case of cold weather. He then pulled slowly out of the parking lot. Made sure his headlights were on. Didn't want to give a cop any stupid reason to pull him over.

Remembering that not far away on the west side and barely inside the perimeter and outside his normal haunts, that there were some industrial areas, he pointed the cute, eco-friendly, corpse carrying coffin, west.

Maintaining his speed at one mile per hour below the changing posted speed limits, twenty minutes later Bad Penny found what he was seeking.

A mixed use industrial park with a dumpster to one end, next to a granite quarry. Stone Mountain's lithic base extended underground for sixty or more miles in every direction so quarries were abundant in north Georgia. With a little luck the remains of a body might not be found in a quarry for days.

He pulled up in front of the business park. *"Dumpster, quarry, dumpster, quarry?"*

It had seen better days. Or maybe it hadn't.

A year ago, Bad Penny had dumped a body in a dumpster. This time, the quarry won out. *"Must continue to be creative and artistic. Besides, probably not a good idea to do it the same way again just so the fucking cops won't get any ideas."*

He'd already noticed a three-foot long heavy chain with huge links hanging loose on the gate next door. Someone had apparently neglected to lock up properly. Good luck for Bad Penny.

At almost midnight he wasn't worried that someone might come around although it was possible a night watchman could be on duty. He hopped out, swung the gate wide, got back in the car, turned off the headlights and scratched off as fast as the little four cylinder hybrid could go.

Bad Penny weighed being there too long against taking enough time to find the perfect spot. Without headlights shining on the quarry he paralleled what he guessed from the pile of stone ahead of him was the quarry's deepest part. Locating a suitable spot, Bad Penny scruffed to a stop, red stained gravel and red Georgia clay flying. When he reached over to pop the passenger door it opened to reveal nothing but air below. Perfect position to dump the body. He retrieved his jacket from where it covered the body first, and was lifting the form from the floorboard to the seat to push it into freefall, when Millie moaned. Her face was a death mask but obviously not quite there. Not a big deal, for when she hit the bottom of the two hundred plus feet deep granite-faced drop she would be way past dead.

As he shoved her out the open door it started to snow, with large, wet, white flakes collecting on the windshield.

The little Prius had gotten noticeably colder while he had the door open. He turned the temperature control on the heater up before pulling away with his headlights still turned off.

***

"Son of a bitch." Ramsey was pissed, again.

"I know. Number six."

"Looks like the mother fucker tried to strangle her, and didn't get the job done, so he dumped her off a cliff."

"She was older than his usual. Bless her heart. I bet she was scared half to death."

"He has no usual. She was available."

"We need to know where that was. It's too bad Wheeling lost him. But, hey, you don't think we're barking up the wrong tree with Wentworth, do you?"

"Are you kidding? I'm more convinced than ever that it's him.

"Okay, so here's the sixty-four-thousand-dollar question. Was he faking the Bad Penny character before, or has BP come back?"

"I don't give a fuck. It doesn't fucking matter to me. I'm just pissed off that his asshole lawyer could convince the Conviction Appeal Commission of the great state of Georgia that that son of a bitch should have been set free."

"I hear you, brother. You know how those bleeding heart defense lawyers are though. But we still don't have a shred of evidence, so it's just our suspicions until we get some."

"So, that's what we have to fucking do."

***

Depressed over the previous night's activity, Pennington couldn't even drag himself out of bed.

"Dude, get up. I need some coffee."

What are you talking about? You're the reason I don't feel like getting up.

"Are you kidding me? You and I are a helluva team."

You and I are not a team. We've never been a team. We're never going to be a team. You got that?

"Whatev. Don't get your boxers in a bunch—ha. Of course with you maybe it should be your panties in a pinch."

When Pennington did finally get up he forced his used-up body into the shower and washed the blonde color out of his hair. He liked the look, but figured it couldn't hurt to get rid of it in case people remembered Millie had been talking to a blonde haired guy.

He tousled his hair with a towel, then slipping on his winery-logo bathrobe with his hair still damp, he picked up his ipad from where he charged it overnight and looked at Atlanta news sites to see if there were any reports about a body at the quarry.

None yet; though it might be a little soon, and he had hope that it would take them a few days to find it. Of course the news media could be working with law enforcement to hush it up for awhile.

***

For the next week Pennington somehow managed to keep Bad Penny at bay, or maybe he just didn't encounter any of the typical triggers that set him off. He did nothing but go to Mass on Sunday, Alon's for coffee a few of the mornings and back to the mall, this time Perimeter Mall in Dunwoody. Trying not to put himself in situations that would tempt Bad Penny.

So much for that. He spotted Gage surreptitiously tailing him and Bad Penny started to rear his ugly head.

He ignored Gage until he could't.

"So, Wentworth, how you doin'? You aren't having anymore fun without me, are you?"

Pennington said, "With all due respect, Mr. Gage, would you just please leave me alone?"

"Well, that's kind of rude. I was keeping an eye on you for Orpheus."

"I'm better off without you keeping an eye on me and I don't think Orpheus, God Bless him, would appreciate what you bring out of me."

With that, Gage disappeared. Pennington had been able to withdraw from him without incident.

Among the huge crowds less than two weeks before Christmas, Bad Penny was able to restrain himself, knowing that it would be difficult to indulge in his particular sort of mayhem without drawing the attention of law enforcement or at the very least, armed mall security.

Pennington spent his days working out in the condo fitness center. He spent his nights watching Christmas specials on television and drinking wine and dining at non-descript nearby eateries. But a week before Christmas he decided to start visiting some of the well known sites again.

This time he decided on another Atanta landmark, the Peachtree Westin Hotel, the tallest hotel in the Western Hemisphere. The revolving Sundial restaurant on top of the cylindrical hotel, was on the seventy-first floor. Its bar was a level higher. Lunch seventy-one floors above Peachtree Street and high above the center of commerce, rotating at six degrees per minute, one revolution per hour, sounded like a good idea

The glass elevator on the building's exterior one could ride to get to the popular restaurant was not for the faint of heart. The view of the concrete city and the surrounding verdant countryside was spectacular but could also be frightening.

After choosing to take it to the top Pennington almost immediately regretted it, as his stomach got a little uneasier with every foot of the rise. When he shakily exited into the restaurant he recognized the setting for various movies and television shows that had been filmed at the famous Atlanta site.

He walked to the hostess stand and asked her to seat him on the empty side of the restaurant. At roughly six degrees per minute he could get a three-hundred-sixty-degree view in about an hour.

He sat a small round table right beside the curved window that was currently looking to the west over the Georgia Dome and the new Mercedes Benz Stadium with the retractable roof, home of the National Football League's Atlanta Falcons. On the restaurant sound system, Mel Torme sang The Christmas Song, almost immediately bringing him to tears since it was his late father's favorite holiday song, one which Pennington remembered him singing to his mother. It caused him to miss them both terribly.

A cute blonde server wearing a nametag reading SHERRY filled his water glass.

"Thank you, darling."

"You're welcome, sir. Would you like something else to drink?"

"Do you have a Napa chard?"

"How does Chalk Hill sound?"

"Sounds like a winner. Let's do it."

Young Sherry grinned, pleased with herself that he was happy with her suggestion.

"Be right back," she said as she turned toward the bar that was in the center and didn't rotate with the rest of the restaurant.

A moment later the cute server returned with a generous pour of the award-winning Napa Valley white.

Since he hadn't had a glass of Chalk Hill in awhile, Pennington leaned back to take a healthy taste, and savor how good it was.

"Do you know what you want to eat or do you need another minute?"

Setting the menu aside, he said, "Cobb Salad. With honey mustard on the side?" He'd returned to his habit of saying it with an inflection at the end, as if it were a question, trying to be nice, instead of barking it like an order like he did in prison.

Sitting on the backside of the revolving dining room, he was virtually alone in the large restaurant.

Fifteen minutes and a quarter rotation later, Sherry returned with his salad, and topped off his water.

"Can I have another glass of the Chalk Hill?'

"Of course."

She returned a moment later with it.

Like the bar, the restrooms were in the center of the restaurant and didn't revolve. A young man, very well dressed and roughly his age walked toward the mens' room and stared at Pennington as he entered.

Upon exiting the young man winked at him.

Bad Penny acknowledged him by raising two fingers.

The guy walked over. "Mind if I join you?"

"Damn. Son of a bitch thinks we're gay."

"Not at all."

He pulled out the chair opposite and slid in.

"I'm Warren."

"Francis, pleased to meet you." And they shook hands across he small table. Harvey stroked Francis-Pennington's palm with his index finger, indicating gay interest.

Bad Penny became enraged and with the rest of the lunchtime crowd on the other side of the restaurant, and not thinking of the consequences, he put both hands on the lip of the small table heaving it into Warren's chest, pinning him, then followed it with a barrage of lefts and rights to his face crushing his nose, and breaking most of his teeth. Then, before anyone on the other side of the restaurant could react or even hear, Bad Penny hefted the table and smashed the floor to ceiling curved window, then picking up Warren, threw him through the opening, to the street seventy-one floors below. His limp body crashed onto the roof of a black stretch limousine setting off the car's alarm. Andrew Young Boulevard, bustling with midday pedestrian and vehicle traffic immediately became impassable during the noontime rush with a huge crowd of onlookers. As the crowd spread, a passing car, going too fast and unable to avoid her, hit a young businesswoman, a consultant for Ernst & Young, killing her immediately. With the wind from such a precipitous height rushing in through the broken window, making it a bad idea, Bad Penny resisted the urge to look to the street below, and beat a hasty exit toward the building's interior elevators, hoping to get lost in the large hotel's throngs while shouting, "A man just jumped through the window. It was horrible. Get out of my way. I need to get to the men's room. I'm going to be sick."

The portals right next to each other, he pushed the button to call the elevator, then ducked in the restroom, standing quietly next to the door to listen for the muffled ding of the elevator bell.

On the elevator for the long ride to the lobby; *you son of a bitch. I'm sick of you.*

"Come on, man. He thought we were gay. We had to do it." It appeared the ends justified the means to Bad Penny.

Stop saying "we." 'We" didn't murder that poor man in the most horrible way possible…you did.

"Well, we'll just have to agree to disagree."

The elevator stopped about half way down and a family—husband, wife and two little girls—got on. The next time the bell dinged it indicated arrival at the lobby.

As Pennington exited the lift, he covered his face and stifled a fake sneeze with his hand, and turned his head away from a platoon of first responders, police, fire and medical personnel, who were rushing to get on.

He walked the perimeter of the large lobby locating a seldom used dark and damp smelling utility stairwell that would take him to the second level of the parking garage. Less likely that anyone else would use such a depressed access.

In his car with a backdrop of lighthearted seasonal music he thought: *You and I have got to have a serious talk.*

"What's up?"

If you don't cut this shit out I'm going to have to take drastic measures.

"Dude, I'm not worried. You don't want to go back to prison either."

I'm not talking about prison.

He didn't respond. Bad Penny seemed to be pissed off.

It appeared to Pennington that he was almost able to summon Bad Penny if he wanted to…and even more importantly erect a wall when he didn't want the evil entity to read his thoughts. Or worse, visit his brain. All he had to do was think of classical music and hum it to himself before thinking about anything he didn't want Bad Penny to know and he was shut out.

***

Tiring of his coffee and his cooking, on Saturday, Pennington decided to go to Alon's for breakfast.

He ordered a large, skim milk latte with two Stevias and, choosing to eat healthy, had a bowl of oatmeal with real butter, brown sugar, mixed berries and real maple syrup. As he lustily dug in, a pretty young brunette sitting a couple tables over smiled at him. He nodded back.

She rose to leave but paused by his table to speak.

"Hi, I'm Cheryl."

"Francis." He rose halfway to shake her hand. "Pleased to meet you."

"Nice to meet you."

"Do you live in the neighborhood?"

"Yes. You?"

"Buckhead—not far."

"Look, here's my card. I don't have time to chat. I sell real estate. Call me sometime. I have to run. I have my ex-husband's dead body in my trunk."

"Excuse me?"

"I'm sorry. I have my ex-husband's ashes in my trunk. He didn't have anyone, so even though we were divorced I told him I would take care of it. I'm on my way up to the north Georgia Mountains to spread them in the place he loved so much."

"I have to admit I was thinking something else entirely. But, I shouldn't joke about it. That's very nice of you."

"It's the least I can do. I'm afraid I broke his heart when I left. Anyway, call me."

***

"That son of a bitch," Ramsey said. I was hoping he'd take a break for Christmas.

"I don't know. I'm beginning to have my doubts about it being him."

"Well I just don't think that guy committed suicide at The Sundial. It just seems like something Wentworth would do. And Cassius lost him again that morning. Apparently he's a madman behind the wheel, even in the ATL's traffic. And we're left with egg on our faces, and that pisses me off. We're making the whole department look bad."

"Well you're right about that, whoever is committing the murders."

***

Pennington spent the next week getting ready for Christmas by listening to Christmas music while cleaning house, baking, and drinking eggnog. He had an old family recipe he made with eggs, real cream, cinnamon, containing light and dark rum, 151 proof and 90 proof, and spiced rum. His father made him promise he'd never share it because when Pennington was in college his father would have spun in his grave if a mob of frat boys had tried and ruined it.

The city had a buzz like no other time of year. Already known for some of the worst traffic in the country, it was amped to a level of insanity at Christmas like most drivers have never experienced, Most of the malls put out orange barrels at their entrances and directed traffic a certain direction in an attempt to minimize disruption to traffic flow.

Pennington went to the mall just to enjoy the joviality of the Christmas season. He loved everything about it—cold weather, Christmas trees, decorations, little kids sitting on Santa Claus' lap. He recalled when his sainted mother had taken him to see Santa to give him his list. The jolly old elf had scared him shitless. Literally. As a little tyke he got so scared he couldn't control his bowels. Santa surely had to take the red suit directly to the cleaners.

At home, he had to open a pile of Christmas cards, then enter the addresses in his journal and started addressing his cards. Thinking ahead, he'd bought them weeks before, a beautiful card with a midnight blue nighttime scene of Bethlehem, with a glittery silver star showing the way to the manger, then almost waited too late to get them in the mail, but hopefully people would understand. He couldn't neglect his friends, his doctor, dentist, insurance agent, or investment advisor and probably more important than anyone, Ben Wasserman, the defense attorney who stopped his execution and got him freed from prison, or he'd be living it down all next year.

Tiring after an hour and a half, he picked up his phone and keyed the number "one" for his best friend. "Ash, I know we haven't talked about it in a few weeks, but you're still coming for Christmas Eve dinner, aren't you?"

"Are you still cooking? And baking?"

"Of course."

"Then, of course I'm coming."

"Great, 7ish? Then I'll go to midnight mass. You're welcome to join me if you like."

"Maybe, I will, Pennington. Maybe, I will."

Clicking off, he momentarily let down his interior guard.

"She's a hottie. Have you ever tried to get anywhere with her?"

Hell, no. She's my best friend. I wouldn't dream of it.

"Okay, okay. I'm just saying."

Well don't. Just don't.

***

Christmas Eve afternoon and listening to Christmas music on a beautiful crisp, holiday eve he was all done with his cleaning, cooking, and baking and after lighting and strategically placing some scented candles—pine, cinnamon and what the candlemaker called a Yule scent, around the living room and kitchen, he sat down with a glass of the traditional family eggnog, to rest awhile before getting himself ready.

Suddenly hopping up, "Oh, damn.", *I almost forgot. My stocking.* He found it in his armoir, he was flooded with sad...and happy, memories. His mother had made it for him—a beautiful needlepoint stocking with a colorful picturesque scene of Santa peeking around a Christmas tree surrounded by toys.

He was in college when she made it and at the time he thought he was too old for what he thought was a childish token, but since she and his father had been killed in the car accident not long after that it quickly became one of his most prized rememberances of her. Both of his parents loved Christmas and although sometimes it was difficult for him to recall their faces, it was easy for him to picture them buzzing around their home frantically, while waiting for the appointed hour. It was the reason he now felt the same way about the season.

The kitchen smelled delicious but was hot from all the cooking and especially baking, Pennington had been doing. So, getting the Bose Sounddock Ashley bought him with his Christmas iPod already inserted, he went outside and set it on a table to cool off with a glass of eggnog and enjoy his favorite music in the sunny, but seasonably chilly weather.

He sat in a chaise and imagined Santa and his sleigh pulled by eight tiny reindeer, flying over the North Georgia Mountains

I wonder what Christmas specials will be on tv tonight. It doesn't matter. I'm going to mass anyway. Hopefully there will some good ones on tomorrow.

After the eggnog and the delightful music of The Nutcracker, he fell asleep in the elongated chair. The last cogent thought he could recall was thinking, *Tchaikovsky, my God, what a genius.*

He woke about five pm shivering and needing to pee.

With darkness encroaching, he turned on the colorful lights of the tree on the terrace, picked up the Sounddock, went back in, peed, and went straight to the shower.

Except for Bad Penny periodically rearing his ugly head he was content back in the world he loved, among the people that for the most part he cared about and cared about him.

He took a shower, using all of his favorite skin conditioners, emollients, lotions and products that made him feel good about himself. Using his razor with the five blades, made of German steel, he shaved under the jets of hot water.

Out of the shower, he brushed, flossed and gargled. He dressed in khaki worsted wool Polo slacks which he paired with a starched white dress shirt covered by a heavy, hand-knitted, Navy blue, donegal wool v-neck sweater to protect against what was sure to be a cold night, with Trask cordovan-colored oxford shoes. He was glad the Catholic Church had relaxed its dress codes for mass even if people still tended to dress more for Christmas and Easter than at other times of year. In the heat of Georgia summers, some people, men and women alike, would even wear shorts to Saturday Vigil mass. He thought God had more important things to worry about than what one wore to celebrate mass.

Looking in the full length mirror on the back of his master bathroom door, he thought, *it's too bad Ashley and I aren't a couple because I'm irresistible tonight.*

"That's what I'm talking about."

I thought you had gone somewhere else. Forget you ever heard it. It was just a statement about how good I look.

"I'm not going anywhere, brother. We're bound together."

Yeah, well, I've got my own ideas about that.

After showering, attending to his rituals and dressing, he had thirty minutes to spare before Ashley was supposed to arrive. He started the Christmas music again, relit the cinnamon candle that had gone out when he opened and reopened the door to the terrace and the ever-present wind on the twenty-fourth floor and fluffed the pillows on the sofa.

At five minutes until seven the doorbell rang.

"Merry Christmas, Ash. Come in."

"Thanks, Pennington. Same to you," she said, handing him a bottle of Dom Perignon champagne. She looked cute in a plaid wool skirt in the colors of winter and a muted orange sweater. Pennington thought they looked like Saks. Knowing how frugal Ashley was she probably got the outfit at the local outlet store.

"And put this under the tree," she said as she handed him a medium size beautifully wrapped box." He placed it next to Ashley's gift.

"Ash, you shouldn't have. Or the bubbly either. It's too much. But I'm glad you did."

"Nonsense. It's Christmas and a special dinner requires a special wine. And I had to get you something. We missed last Christmas— Oops. Sorry."

"Don't worry about it. We did miss last Christmas. I don't even remember where I was. And, I agree with you about the champagne. Why don't I pour us a wee glass to sip while I get the food on the table?"

Bing Crosby's *White Christmas* was playing.

Pennington retrieved a hand towel with which to twist the cork so it wouldn't fly away when he freed it. The towel read in cursive script,

"I wish there was more wine in a bottle so there'd be enough for two people." A moment later, a gentle pop and some of the bubbly erupted softly from the bottle's confines.

Pouring a small amount into two flowered wine flutes—treasured family heirlooms—he handed one to Ashley as O Holy Night by Trans-Siberian Orchestra gave a heavy metal edge to their Christmas.

"I love TSO," said Ashley, using the abbreviation their biggest fans used.

They touched glasses. "Merry Christmas, Ash."

"Merry Christmas, Pennington." Each took a sip.

"I haven't had Dom in a very long time. I'd forgotten how wonderful it is. Thanks again, Ash."

"You're very welcome. It is lovely, isn't it?"

Pennington started covering the dining table with platters and bowls—sides of sweet potato casserole, cranberries, dressing, mash potatoes, green beans, corn casserole, before he presented the turkey. He placed bottles of white bordeaux and French rose' on the table

"By the way, the chard or the rose' either one, should be great with turkey."

"Your table looks beautiful. I love the mismatched red globe wine glasses."

"Thanks. I've bought them at antique stores whenever I've come across them for years."

Finally, he brought out the big bird on a large dish and said proudly, "The *sine qua non* of the Christmas dinner."

"Without which there is nothing," Ashley said.

"You remember your Latin."

"Mrs. Driscoll wouldn't be happy with me if I didn't. And it's beautiful, besides."

"Thanks, Ash. It's a Martha Stewart recipe that I doctored up. You soak a cheesecloth in Chardonnay and melted butter and baste the turkey with it while continuing to add more chard and butter."

"How could it be bad—cooked in Chardonnay and butter? I'm sure Martha would approve."

"Thanks, I hope so. You know she's the only who understands dressing vs stuffing."

"What?"

"She accurately says "If you cook it inside the turkey, it's stuffing;

if you cook it in a casserole dish it's dressing." You'd think if she understands that, being a Yankee, everybody else could get it."

As Ashley tried a bite of his "dressing" she said, "anyway your dressing is to die for."

"Thanks, Ash. It's my favorite part of Christmas dinner."

"Mine, too."

"By the way, are you going to your mom's for dinner tomorrow?"

"Yes, you know since their divorce I alternate holidays between mom and dad. I have to admit I'm glad it's mom's turn. The Thanksgiving turkey at dad's was dry and I think he bought the sides and pumpkin pie at a supermarket. They certainly weren't like this. And at least mom can cook."

"Thanks, but I'm sure your mom's will be fine. I remember when I would come home with you from school sometimes. She always felt like she had to feed us and she was a fine cook."

"What are you going to do?"

"Probably won't leave home. Cook breakfast. Watch Christmas specials and movies on tv. Just enjoy the day.

"That sounds good. By the way, what do you think of the rash of murders being committed?"

He made a face. "I don't want to talk about it, Ash. It upsets me too much. Besides, it's Christmas Eve. Let's talk about more pleasant things."

"Of course you're right."

"So, which wine would you like?"

"I think I'll have another small glass of champagne before I switch." So Pennington poured her more Dom.

Noticing her plate when he poured, he asked, "How about some more dressing?"

"I'd love some."

"Good, because I would, too."

"And, I could have some of the rose' now."

"Coming up. And I'll have some of the white bordeaux."

"By the way, is the New Year's Eve party still on?"

"I was planning on sending out email reminders the day after Christmas."

"I can help you with that if you like. I'm off work the day after, too."

"I'd love for you to."

"I still have the list from the fall party, so I'll start in the morning the day after tomorrow."

"Excuse me just a minute." He went over to the Christmas iPod and clicked it.

"I love the Charlie Brown Christmas. All the piano music is by the Vince Guaraldi Trio."

"Oh, I love that, too. The sounds of the piano echoed delightfully off the wood floors.

"It's a shame. He died way too young. I think he was forty-seven."

"Yes it is. But enough of terrible."

"How about dessert—pumpkin pie or dark chocolate bourbon/pecan pie?"

"I think just a sliver of pumpkin."

Pennington got a slice of the pumpkin for Ashley and a piece of bourbon-pecan for himself.

"Oh, that's too big, Pennington. Half that," Ashley said.

Ignoring her he said, "A nice red would be good with dessert. Let me get one from the wine room."

Returning with a bottle and two new glasses, he said, "I think you'll like this Napa Cabernet."

"I'm sure I will. You know I trust you when it comes to wine."

After a bite of pumpkin pie she drew in a mouthful of the red wine. "This is wonderful."

"Thanks, Ash. My paternal grandmother's recipe. I called her nana. She passed when I was in high school, so you never met her."

"Well, I'm glad she gave you her recipe."

"Me, too. Are you going to mass with me?"

"If you still want me to."

"Of course I do, but I should probably get this food put away."

"Let me help. It'll go faster."

They covered dishes of food—there were a lot of them—and pies, and put them in the Viking refrigerator. Good thing it was so large. And Pennington put Christmas wine bottle toppers in the mostly unfinished bottles.

"Oh, and you need to open your gift before we leave," Pennington said.

"And you, too."

"Come on," he said as he walked toward the tree.

Ashley joined him as he picked up both gifts and they sat next to each other on the sofa.

"You, first," said Pennington.

"Let's open them at the same time,"

"Sounds good," he said as he started tearing into the beautiful wrapping job.

Ashley opened hers more gently.

"Ash, you shouldn't have," he said when he saw the beautiful buttery soft camel-colored leather driving gloves. "The champagne and these are way too much."

"What about my gift? A Neiman Marcus cashmere sweater. Pennington, this must have cost a fortune. But the tan color will go with my outfit." And she draped it around her neck and over one shoulder. "How's it look?"

"Beautiful. Check the mirror. And who am I going to spend my money on, anyway? It was sitting there earning interest the entire time I was in…that place. I couldn't have spent any if I'd wanted to. But, we need to leave if we're going to make it to mass on time."

***

All Saints Catholic Church was his family's parish when Pennington was a boy. They arrived early at eleven thirty p.m. because Pennington had always liked hearing the full orchestra playing Christmas carols until midnight.

"Boy this place brings back memories," he whispered to Ashley as they entered. It had hardly changed. "And I've always loved the spicy smell of frankincense."

"Do you remember what happened the last time you and I were in church together?"

You son of a bitch, don't make me swear in church. I'm still trying to forget that. How dare you show up here, now, in this holy place, at Jesus' birth. You have no right.

At midnight, mass began with the Monsignor welcoming the people, then he blessed the crib in the nativity Scene, before the liturgy, and the Gospel followed by prayers. After carols and more prayers there was communion, and the mass was ended. The celebration lasted longer than masses at other times of the year.

***

Pennington and Ashley split the list of email addys to send out the reminder-invitations. Christmas over, Pennington got up early and started coffee before getting his iPad to send the emails. If everyone showed up that said they would, it would be a great party to usher in the New Year and watch all the fireworks.

Chapter Thirteen
The Inglorious End

For such a large gathering, Pennington again borrowed Ashley's housekeeper, Mirka.

So she could enjoy her holiday, Mirka arrived on December thirtieth. Pennington would just have to keep his house clean for an extra day before the party.

Virtually everybody he'd invited had committed to being there.

Eight o' clock and people began arriving. As a mix of popular and Christmas played—Goo Goo Dolls followed by "It's Christmas In New York" from Radio City Music Hall Christmas Spectacular, which Pennington's family used to go to New York for every year—he and Ashley put coats in the office, an erstwhile bedroom.

"Brook, Warner, welcome. How was your Christmas." "Beautiful, Pennington, beautiful; how was yours?" Brook answered for them.

Ashley and Brook bussed in the way of Europeans: on both cheeks.

Warner, wanting to be cool, but never quite succeeding, fist-bumped Pennington but positioned his fist horizontally instead of vertically. Pennington gave him points for the attempt.

"That guy sure thinks he's cool, doesn't he?"

Give him a break. He can't help it. Why don't you just disappear?

Talon and Lace were late arriving since they had to see off visiting family.

Worried, Talon said, "Pennington, what time do the fireworks start?"

"We've got plenty of time. About eleven thirty so they can do the finales at straight up midnight."

On New Year's Eve the guys wanted to watch football. Because New Year's Eve was on Sunday, though, they had to watch NFL games. The usual bowl games would be on New Year's Day. Like at the last party, they watched them muted and listened to music and carried on conversations.

Once again, the women encircled the table of food, making plates of food for husbands or boyfriends, while drinking wine.

An old Pennington friend, Jefferson, was more interested in

Pennington's book collection than the game. His partner, Harry, was hanging out with the women.

At halftime of the Falcons and Panthers game the men convened to the terrace for a quick cigar. The outdoor area was bathed in color by the bright lights of the outdoor Christmas tree. It was but a few puffs and a short time later that Ashley stuck her head out the door. "The game's coming back on."

Cigars were extinguished and the guys returned to Bruce Springsteen singing *Santa Claus is Coming To Town.*

About the time the game ended, Pennington said, "We should probably go outside. All the displays will be starting." So, men and women alike, exited for the terrace. Five minutes later, the first rumblings of explosions began.

"Look, there's one." The first starburst of the night, a large bright green one, exploded over Roswell. It was immediately followed by another green one that looked like it was over Alpharetta and gold and red ones over suburbs further north. Then, one after another followed as fast as one could look, in everyone direction, over every city and neighborhood in the north burbs.

"Ooh, ahh," everyone sounded in unison. "Look, look."

Dense fog covered the ground between every treeline and snow began to fall. Surprisingly, especially in the south, the heavy snow was accompanied by thunder.

As the various fireworks displays slowed down, a blanket of smoke settled over the forests of north Georgia. It was shortly after midnight, the new year's birth.

The new year arrived, and just after midnight the rapid-fire stoccato of explosions slowed to a stop.

Pennington said, "You're all welcome to stay longer but that's probably the end of the free show."

After a few minutes of energetic chatter, congratulations, individualized thank yous, and indefinite promises to get together soon, real soon, the partygoers started to depart. All started to leave except his best friend, Ashley. "Pennington, can I stay over?" I could sleep on the couch."

"Nonsense, Ash. I'll sleep on the sofa. You can sleep in my bed. Mirka made it with clean sheets yesterday.

"Thanks, Pennington. I just would rather not drive in the traffic on

New Year's Eve after drinking."

"I insist on it."

Ashley went to the master bedroom and closed the door.

Pennington decided to have one last glass, a very important one, perhaps the most important one of his life, a Caymus cab, out on the terrace. He contemplated Bushido and its seven principles and as he sipped he recalled what Orpheus told him of Socrates' thoughts about death: Philosophers should welcome and could even benefit from death, although he didn't approve of suicide. Thinking of himself as the philosophical scion of the great one, he could only hope that the man who had influenced millions would approve of what he was about to do.

And he knew without doubt from his weeks of training with Gage that the man was somewhere below, keeping a watchful eye on him on behalf of Orpheus.

"That was a real nice party dude. We could have done some real damage, though."

That will never happen again.

"What are you talking about? You know you can't stop me."

Watch me.

Pennington set the glass of fine red wine on a small table between the two chaises, rose and walked toward the wall of his terrace.

"Wait. Stop. What are you doing? You can't do this."

It's the only thing I can do.

"You're a coward."

Quite the contrary, this is the bravest thing I've ever done. I'm thinking clearer now than I have since the first time you arrived. Tonight you and I truly become one. Socrates would understand that I'm not really killing myself, but killing you. May God have mercy on my soul.

"No matter what you do, don't forget. You're still a pussy."

Pennington started his climb over the stucco terrace wall. A last glance at the brightly-colored Christmas tree, and he plunged into the dark dead of night. It embraced the darkness in his soul.

www.ingramcontent.com/pod-product-compliance
Lightning Source LLC
Chambersburg PA
CBHW020124180626
46810CB00004B/1400